"I'm not sure how to say this."

Anna leaned forward. "Just start at the beginning."

"I haven't told anyone, but the first time I saw Frank Daggett was the day August and I had dinner with Gustaf and Olina."

"I didn't know that." Anna leaned back and smiled.

"He was coming down the stairs in the hotel lobby while we were waiting for Gustaf and Olina to arrive. I glanced up," Gerda said as a blush moved up her cheeks, "and when our eyes met, it was as if everything within me connected with everything in him. I don't know how to explain it. For a moment, I felt as if we were the only two people in the room."

Anna looked as if she were holding back a chuckle. "That's interesting."

Gerda got up and walked to the window nearest the sewing machine. She held back the curtain and gazed at nothing in particular. "Don't you see? All these years I've waited for God to bring me someone to love, and the only person I've felt anything special for is a man who isn't a Christian. I've been praying for God to take the temptation from me. I just can't get too close to him, because. . ."

After a moment, Anna asked, "Because what?"

Gerda turned away and crossed her arms. "I'm afraid I could fall in love with him very easily. I can't risk that."

LENA NELSON DOOLEY is a free-lance author and editor who lives with her husband in Texas. During the twenty years she has been a professional writer, she has been involved as a writer or editor on a variety of projects. She developed a seminar called "Write Right," and she hosts a writing critique group in her home. She presently works full-time as an author and editor. She has a dramatic ministry, an international speaking ministry that crosses denominational lines, and an international Christian clowning ministry. When she and her husband vacation in Mexico, they enjoy visiting and working with missionary friends. Her Web site is www.LenaNelsonDooley.com.

Books by Lena Nelson Dooley

HEARTSONG PRESENTS
HP54—Home to Her Heart
HP492—The Other Brother
HP584—His Brother's Castoff
HP599—Double Deception

Don't miss out on any of our super romances. Write to us at the following address for information on our newest releases and club information.

Heartsong Presents Readers' Service
PO Box 719
Uhrichsville, OH 44683

Or visit www.heartsongpresents.com

Gerda's
Lawman

Lena Nelson Dooley

To Gail,
Enjoy !!
Philippians 3:10
Lena Nelson
Dooley

Heartsong Presents

This book is dedicated to my youngest granddaughter, Amanda. You are a joy and treasure. I look forward to seeing what God is going to do in your life. And every book is dedicated to my husband, James, who has showered me with his love for most of my life.

A note from the Author:
I love to hear from my readers! You may correspond with me by writing:

Lena Nelson Dooley
Author Relations
PO Box 719
Uhrichsville, OH 44683

ISBN 1-59310-250-X

GERDA'S LAWMAN

Our mission is to publish and distribute inspirational products offering exceptional value and biblical encouragement to the masses.

All Scripture quotations are taken from the King James Version of the Bible.

PRINTED IN THE U.S.A.

Or check out our Web site at www.heartsongpresents.com

one

April 1896

Frank Daggett sure hoped that was a town up ahead and not a mirage. He had been in the saddle so long he felt as if it were fused to the seat of his pants. Finally, he could have a bath, a shave, a hot meal, and a real bed. In that order. But the long ride had been worth it. Although he was bone weary, he could sense that indefinable excitement he always felt when he was about to catch his prey. Pierre Le Blanc and his daughter had to be just ahead. His two daughters, if Frank had it figured right. Litchfield, Minnesota, was the end of the line. For him and for the Le Blancs—in more ways than one.

Litchfield looked like a nice enough town, and Frank hoped it wouldn't take very long to bring the Le Blancs to justice. He was ready to get on with his life, and he couldn't until he had finished this one chore. Although he was only thirty years old, he felt ancient. He had seen enough to age him beyond his years. Bad people and their evil deeds had hardened him so much he hardly knew who he was anymore—certainly not the idealistic young man who became a U.S. Marshal all those years ago. He didn't even know where he belonged. Maybe when he finished this quest he could find out. For the first time in over ten years, he could have a life of his own, complete with a home and family, like most men his age.

Because of his obsession with catching Pierre Le Blanc and his daughters, he was no longer a marshal. The Old Man had given him a choice: Give up this pursuit or turn in his badge. The head of the U.S. Marshals taught Frank everything he knew about being a lawman. And like all of the marshals, he had tremendous respect for his superior. Frank had only disagreed with the Old Man about one thing—his decision that the U.S. Marshals would stop pursuing the Le Blancs.

With great reluctance, Frank had removed the star. Since then, he had been on his own as he followed the trail of this confidence man and his family. It was a good thing that Frank had saved so much of his pay over the years and his needs were negligible. A lot of his money remained in a bank back East, waiting for him to get to the point where he could start living a real life. He wouldn't have to worry about finances while he was establishing himself.

Sometimes he had been so close to catching these criminals that he could almost taste victory. But he always arrived after they had left the vicinity. Then it would take him awhile to find their trail again. They committed crimes in such a way that no one could prove they did it. That was why Frank had finally figured out there had to be two girls. And they must be twins to look that much alike. It was the only way they could have pulled off so many seemingly perfect crimes. But Frank knew that there were no perfect crimes. It was about time this family was brought to justice, and he was the man to do that very thing.

Frank stopped his horse in front of the first hotel he came to. He looked up at the second-story windows. They even sported curtains. It was a high-class establishment—nicer than many of the places he had stayed during this long quest. After tying the reins of his mount to the hitching post, he removed his saddlebags from the horse and slung them across his shoulder. He stepped up on the high boardwalk without bothering to go down to where steps had been built. His legs were long enough, and he was too tired to go even that much farther. The steady beat of his boots on the boards and the jingle of his spurs accompanied him through the door. His whole body itched and he was eager to remove his traveling gear and put on clean clothes.

A young man sat behind the hotel's front desk, writing something in a book. His head was bent forward, and Frank was sure the man didn't even know anyone was around until Frank dropped his saddlebags on the counter.

"I'd like a room."

The man looked startled as he slammed the book shut and glanced up. He stood and pulled the hotel register from a shelf under the counter. "Do you want a room that looks out on the street or one in the back where it's quieter?"

Frank wished he could say, "In the back," but he needed to be able to keep an eye on the town's comings and goings. That was the only way he could keep a lookout for the Le Blancs. He just hoped this wasn't another town where rowdy cowboys came to drink late into the night.

"In the front would be fine." Frank reached for his wallet. "Do I need to pay now?"

"How long are you staying?" The man smiled up at Frank.

"I'm not really sure. How about if I pay you for a week, and we'll see if I need to be here longer?"

The man pushed the register book toward Frank, handed him a pen, and moved the ink well closer to him. "That would be fine, Mister. . ." He watched as Frank wrote his name. "Daggett. That'll be five dollars for the week. You're in room three." He turned around and retrieved the key from the numbered cubbyhole behind him.

"Where's the best place to get a bath, a shave, and a meal?"

❧

Gerda Nilsson was just putting the finishing touches on her hairdo when August knocked at the door of the apartment. She shoved one last hairpin into the style to anchor it before she answered the door.

"I'm coming." Thick carpet muffled her footsteps as she crossed the parlor. She opened the door and hugged her brother. "Why didn't you just use your key?"

August returned her hug, then stood back. "I only kept the key because you insisted. It's a good idea for me to check on things for you when you're out at the farm, since you're living here alone. But I won't use it for any other reason. You deserve your privacy, too." He looked around the apartment that had also been his wife's home before they married. "I like what you've done with the place. It really expresses your personality."

"Thank you, kind sir." Gerda gave a low curtsy. She and her brother had always enjoyed a playful relationship.

He bowed slightly and nodded. "Are you ready, milady?" August picked up her jacket from the claret-colored velvet settee. He helped her into the wrap, opened the door, and escorted her down the stairs and into the warm spring twilight.

Gerda placed her hand in the crook of his elbow as they walked across the street to the hotel. "It was really nice of Anna to offer to keep Gustaf and Olina's children so we could take them out to dinner for their anniversary."

"She loves those two little ones. *Ja*, for sure. And I do, too. They come over to our house a lot, since we live so close."

When they entered the hotel lobby, Gerda looked around the room. She didn't come here often, but she had always liked the friendly, yet elegant, atmosphere. The gaslights around the walls gave a warm glow to the plush carpeting and matching wallpaper. Several potted plants enhanced the décor's sense of opulence. Whenever she came to the hotel, its air of sophistication made her feel that Litchfield was as cosmopolitan as Chicago or New York City.

Gerda's attention was drawn to a man beginning to descend the stairs. He was taller than any man she had ever seen. Although his body was lean, it was muscular. His face was dark and clean-shaven except for a neat mustache. *He must spend a lot of time in the sun.* The top of his forehead was lighter than the rest of his tanned face, evidence that he wore a cowboy hat most of the time. He wasn't dressed like a cowboy, but as he walked down the stairs, he had that bowlegged gait of a man who spent most of his life on horseback. His luxurious, thick dark hair looked wet and was slicked back, but separate locks were pulling into strong waves as they dried.

For some inexplicable reason, she felt drawn to him. Her fingers tingled with the desire to brush back an errant curl that had drooped over his strong forehead. She had never felt that way about any man. For a moment, she held her breath in wonder. His most arresting feature—his eyes—were a clear, icy blue. When his gaze met hers, something passed between them that was both exciting and disturbing. Uncomfortable, Gerda quickly looked away.

What is wrong with me? Maybe it was because all her friends had soul mates, and she wanted one, too. Why did some stranger affect her this way? Gerda was glad that Gustaf and Olina arrived at that moment, and the four of them went into the dining room. She tried to dismiss the man from her thoughts.

❧

Frank stopped halfway down the stairs. What had just happened? He was going to the hotel restaurant to get something to eat, minding his own business, when a vision of loveliness entered the lobby. Her beauty almost took his breath away. He had seen those new calendars painted by the artist named Gibson. She looked as if she had just stepped out of one. She was the right size with curves in all the right places. Her delicate features proclaimed class and character. Her light blond hair was formed into a poufy style and had a cluster of curls nested in the crown. Curly tendrils brushed her cheeks and neck where he wished he could place his lips. He could just imagine what the silky strands would feel like. He would have to stop thinking like that!

When she looked into his eyes, he had felt something he had never felt before. Something that crackled through the room, almost sucking out all the air leaving nothing to breathe. He wondered if anyone else had sensed it. He glanced around, but no one was paying either of them any attention.

Frank wasn't looking for a relationship yet. If he found one, or one found him, it would have to be a relationship with no strings attached, at least until his mission was over. He wasn't ready to settle down, and that girl had strings dangling off her so long they would really hog-tie a man. Frank almost turned around and went back to his room, but just then his stomach rumbled so loudly he was sure everyone within a mile radius could hear it. He had to get something to eat. If only she and her companions hadn't gone into the dining room.

Frank continued toward the open doorway of the restaurant. His attention was drawn to the table where the woman and her friends were sitting. It was a good thing they were on one side of the room. He would just choose a table on the other side, and that would be the end of it. With the decision made, he looked around the room for an empty table.

He hadn't thought that this town would have many people staying at a hotel, but there were plenty in the restaurant.

Perhaps this is why Le Blanc was here. Evidently, Litchfield had some affluent citizens. Most of these people were dressed in more expensive clothing than he'd seen in many places. Finally, he spied an empty table on the exact opposite side of the room from where the woman and her party sat. With the large dining area separating them, he could almost forget she was there.

However, when Frank walked across the room and selected a place to sit, he chose a chair that gave him a clear view of the beauty. He couldn't take his eyes off of her until the waitress came to take his order.

"My name is Molly." The grandmotherly woman smiled at him. She raised her voice to be heard over the din of voices and silverware clanking against dishes in the background. "You're new to town, aren't you? You look like you could use a good meal."

Frank nodded, ignoring her question. No one needed to know his business. "What do you have?"

While the woman recited a list of items, Frank couldn't keep from glancing at the beauty seated across the room. When Molly stopped talking, all he could remember her saying was "pot roast."

"I'll have the roast beef." Frank looked up into her kind eyes. "It's been a long time since I've had any."

"We get lots of travelers through here." Molly's eyes twinkled as she talked. "They always appreciate a good hot meal." She started to walk off then turned back toward him. "Our cook makes hot rolls that will melt in your mouth. And we have plenty of butter to go with them."

"That'll be better than the hardtack I've been eating." Frank had enough of that in the past few weeks to last a lifetime.

When the waitress went to get him a cup of coffee, he

glanced toward the table where the vision of loveliness sat. Her every move was grace itself. Her dainty hand fluttered like a butterfly on its way to pick up her glass of water. When she turned to speak to the man on her left, she cocked her head toward him, revealing a profile that looked just liked his mother's cameo. It was the only thing he still owned that had belonged to her, and it was precious to him. He kept that cameo locked in a safe-deposit box in the bank where his savings were.

"Here's your coffee, sir." Molly set the steaming china cup and its saucer in front of him. He glanced up at her, almost sorry for the interruption of his thoughts.

"Thank you." At least he was able to remember his manners. He picked up the cup and took a sip. He liked his coffee hot and strong, but not too strong. This coffee was just right. He set the cup down and looked back across the room.

Why did he torture himself this way? That woman had an escort. She might be married. But somehow he didn't think she was. He had spent too many years watching people not to know the signs. And there was no indication that the couple was married or even romantically involved. The other couple at the table was another matter. Marriage screamed from every look and touch they shared.

When Frank glanced around the room again, his gaze stopped on a man who just had to be a banker. No one else in the room wore a waistcoat with a gold watch chain draped across it. Litchfield must have a healthy economy from the looks of this man. Just the kind of town Le Blanc preyed on. Frank wondered if these people had any idea what they were in for. He had to stop the Le Blanc gang before they destroyed any more lives.

His attention quickly returned to the woman sitting across

the room. He couldn't seem to keep his eyes off of her.

"Here you are." The waitress set his meal in front of him. "Some folks say we serve the finest food west of the Mississippi."

"That sounds good to me." Frank smiled up at her before picking up his fork.

Steam rose from the plate, bringing with it the pleasant aroma of roast beef. Carrots and potatoes, covered with a generous helping of a rich, brown gravy, surrounded the meat. There was nothing he liked better than a good gravy. His stomach growled again. This time louder. He hoped the group across the room couldn't hear it.

The first bite was heavenly. He chewed it slowly, savoring the almost forgotten flavors that reminded him of just how much he had given up to bring Le Blanc to justice. He hoped that, at last, this would be the town where he would arrest the man and his daughters.

The waitress returned with a dish of butter and a basket of hot yeast rolls. "Don't forget to save room for dessert. Tonight we have apple pie."

Could life get any better than this? Frank took his time eating. He wanted to enjoy every minute of this good food. But more than that, he decided to just relax and enjoy watching the beautiful woman. Who knew? Someday he would be ready to settle down. Someday maybe he would find a woman much like her to marry.

❧

When they were seated at a table in the dining room, Gerda decided to forget what had happened in the hotel lobby and concentrate on her brothers and sister-in-law. "Well, Olina, I guess it's nice for you to get to go out without the children."

Olina smiled at her. "Oh yes, it is a real treat, for sure. It was good of you and August to plan this little celebration."

"Actually, it was Anna's idea." August picked up his linen napkin and spread it across his lap.

"Why didn't she come with us?" Olina asked.

Gerda laughed. "You mean besides the fact that she's keeping your children for you?" Olina nodded. "I offered to keep them at the apartment, but Anna thought it would be special for Gustaf's brother and sister to take the two of you out."

August picked up his fork and turned it over and over in his hands, as if he were checking its weight. "She really likes having Olga and Sven at the house." He put the fork down and cleared his throat. "She's hoping we'll have a little one ourselves pretty soon. I told her that it has only been a few months since we married, and I enjoy our time together, but I want children pretty soon, too. *Ja*, that's for sure."

Gustaf patted his wife's hand. "Well, we have an announcement to make, and you two will be the first to hear."

Olina blushed and looked down at her plate. "We are going to have another baby this fall."

Gerda got up and went around the table to hug Olina. "I am so happy for you." When she passed Gustaf on the way back to her chair, she hugged him, too. "And I'm happy for you, big brother."

The waitress came to their table. "What are we all having tonight?"

"I think this calls for steaks." August looked at each of them in turn. "Unless you want something else. We have a lot to celebrate."

When the waitress left, conversation flowed around the table, but Gerda's attention was divided. That cowboy was sitting across the room. She could see him when she turned to talk to August. The man seemed to be enjoying his food, but every once in a while, she could feel his gaze on her. Why was he doing that? It made her very uncomfortable. Though she was glad to have this time with her relatives, she couldn't forget the man or the impression he had made on her when they were in the lobby.

It didn't make any sense. She felt drawn to him, even here in the dining room. She was aware when his coffee arrived. While he ate his roast beef and hot rolls, she looked at him from time to time. He had perfect table manners, not like some of the cowboys she had seen. She didn't want him to catch her watching him, so she peeked at him out of the corners of her eyes to make sure it wasn't when he was looking at her.

I am acting like an old maid. Just because everyone else is married doesn't mean anything is wrong with my life, does it? She was a successful proprietor with a comfortable home, good friends, and a family who loved her. But they weren't a husband and children. Then she felt that deep longing she had harbored since she'd become an adult. She wanted to be loved by a man the way *Far* loved *Mor*. The way Gustaf loved Olina. The way August loved Anna. The way Anna's brothers Ollie and Lowell loved their wives. She wanted a home of her own, not just an apartment above a store. And she wanted children. To feel their arms around her neck. . .to have them call her, "Mother." Oh yes, Gerda wanted all those things more than she could tell anyone. *But that cowboy across the dining room is not the man to give them to me.*

two

If Frank had been eating in a tavern or even a small café, he would have lit up a cheroot and enjoyed a smoke with his after-dinner coffee, but it didn't seem like the thing to do in this classy restaurant. He didn't want to leave where he was sitting while that beauty was across the room, so he sipped the hot beverage and relaxed in his chair, taking frequent peeks at her. The waitress had filled his cup three more times before the party he was watching got up and left the room.

When Frank emerged from the restaurant, he felt too restless to sleep. Instead of going to his room, he decided to go outside for a smoke. The sun had set and gaslights flickered along the main street, casting indefinite circles of light at regular intervals along the boardwalk. Frank glanced down the street toward the saloon. Light, noise, and tobacco smoke poured out through the swinging doors. When he was younger, he would have felt drawn to the place, but it held no enticement tonight. He fished in the pocket of his shirt for a cheroot and placed the end between his lips. He then pulled a small box of matches from his vest pocket, withdrew one, and returned the box to his pocket. Leaning down, he struck the matchstick against the sole of his boot and applied the flame to the end of the thin cigar. The smoke curled around his head as he moved down the sidewalk away from the doorway and leaned back against the wall.

He wondered where the sheriff's office was. Tomorrow he would need to find it. Frank decided that he would wait and alert the lawman after he'd found the Le Blancs. At that point, he would need assistance, since he was no longer an officer of the law himself. Frank could see a train station past the end of this block. He wondered how often the train came through town. All the lights were off in the depot, so there must not be any more due tonight.

Frank took another draw on his small cigar. Just then a lamp was lighted in the upstairs room across the street. A large sign spanning the building proclaimed it BRAXTON'S MERCANTILE. One of the downstairs windows at the end of the building had DRESS EMPORIUM painted in letters that matched those on the mercantile sign. An elegant dress in some shimmery fabric the color of rich cream was draped over a dress form in that window. Frank liked women's clothing without too many frills. The clean lines of the garment would look good on the woman he had watched during dinner. Of course, with her classic features and perfect figure, almost anything would look good on her. He wondered if she had seen this dress. He also wondered where she lived and if he would ever see her again. *Probably not, so I should just quit thinking about her.* But he wasn't ready to release her from his thoughts.

Earlier in the day, when Frank took his horse to be stabled at the livery, he'd noticed that the building looked as though it hadn't been there long. The wood was new, not weathered like the smithy that stood nearby. It made him wonder why a town this size hadn't had a livery stable before this. A few questions about the new business might help him open a conversation that would lead to the whereabouts of the Le Blancs.

Frank moved away from the wall and leaned against a post that supported the porch. The night felt chilly. He was tired, but not sleepy. He figured he just might as well go to his room, so he threw the stub of the cigar in the dirt and stepped off the boardwalk to snuff it out with the heel of his boot. He glanced up and down the silent street before he entered the front door to the hotel.

Frank hadn't lost the feeling that he was close to Le Blanc and his daughters, but it wasn't any stronger now than when he'd come into town. He was pretty sure they weren't at this hotel. He hoped he hadn't missed them once again, but he decided not to dwell on that. It would just keep him from being able to sleep tonight.

As he crossed the hotel lobby, the young man behind the desk looked up over the top of his spectacles. "Do you need anything else, Sir?"

"No, thank you. I'm going to turn in for the night." When Frank reached the step on the carpeted stairs where he had first become aware of the woman, he turned and looked at the place where she had stood. He half hoped she would be there now, but that was a crazy thought. As he knew it would be, the spot was empty. So was the rest of the lobby, except for the man behind the desk, who had returned to reading his book.

❧

Gerda was glad to leave the restaurant and get that cowboy out of sight and off her mind. August accompanied her to the door of her apartment. He unlocked the door with his key.

She turned toward her brother and gave him a hug. "Thank you. I'll be fine now."

August looked a little disappointed. He may have wanted to stay and talk awhile, but she was afraid she might blurt out something about that cowboy. Gerda was confident that neither of her brothers had noticed him. She certainly didn't want to call attention to him now.

She was glad she'd left one lamp burning. It gave her enough light to get to the others. For some reason, she didn't want the apartment to be dark tonight.

Gerda walked over to the window and pulled back the curtain. She stayed mostly behind the fabric and looked at the hotel across the street, wondering which room was the cowboy's. *Probably one in the back where it's quieter.* Since they spent so much time out on the range, didn't cowboys like to be away from the noise of town? Unless he had gone down to the saloon. Although he was dressed like a gentleman at dinner, he might have headed that way afterward. For all she knew, he was just a snake in the grass like Pierre Le Blanc. But she hoped not. How could she have felt that strong connection in the hotel lobby if the man was like Pierre?

What if he were something besides a drifter? Could Gerda have a relationship with him? What was she thinking? She didn't know if the man was a Christian or even if he was a decent man. It must have been because of the wedding anniversary and all the talk of children. That was why her thinking had gone awry. She was fine just as she was right now.

Then an image came to mind of her old maid aunt, who had died when Gerda was a little girl. The woman was dried up. Her skin was wrinkled and her outlook on life was sour. Unlike Aunt Ada, Gerda loved children. Just because Gerda wasn't married didn't mean she would end up like her aunt. Besides, maybe God just hadn't yet brought the man into her life that He wanted her to marry.

Gerda released the edge of the curtain with a disgusted sigh, then walked into the parlor and picked up the book of poetry August had brought as a housewarming gift after she and Anna moved into the apartment. She sat in the rocking chair and read a few pages but soon closed the volume. Poetry was not what she needed tonight. Too many of the poems were about love. Maybe she should read the Bible.

When she picked up the leather-bound book, it fell open to Esther. Gerda read all ten chapters. God had Esther marry a king to save His people from destruction. Surely, God had a purpose for keeping Gerda unmarried so long. She wished He would tell her what it was. . .and soon.

"Father God, forgive me for feeling dissatisfied tonight. Please help me wait for Your plan for my life. Help me be happy and patient until You bring something else—and help me recognize what You are doing when You do. Amen." Praying aloud helped God seem more real to Gerda, as if He were sitting on the settee across the room. Although she felt a calmness settle on her spirit, she wished to hear an audible reply from Him.

She hadn't been dissatisfied with her life until that tall, tan, handsome stranger connected with her across the hotel lobby. Gerda thought her prayer had been sincere, but she didn't sleep very soundly that night. She dreamed disturbing things about growing old alone, and the cowboy from the hotel flitted in and out of her nonsensical dreams at odd times and for no apparent reason.

❧

Frank didn't get ready for bed when he went to his room. He didn't even light the lamp. One of the gas streetlights was right outside his window. He didn't pull the shade down, so he could see all he needed from the glow it provided. Frank stood beside the window and studied the area one more time. The lighted windows above the store had curtains on them. It was probably where someone lived. He wondered who. Maybe the owner of the mercantile.

He looked down to the empty street below. When he glanced back across the street, a woman was pulling the shade down on one of the windows. All he could see was her hand and part of her skirt.

Leaning his weight on the hand that rested on the window frame, Frank wondered how long it would be before he could find the Le Blancs. He would make discreet inquiries tomorrow, because he didn't want to alert them that someone was after them. Stepping away from the window, he rubbed his hand through his unruly curls. Sometimes he thought it would be easier to just shave his head when he shaved his face. Then his hair wouldn't be such a problem to control. Maybe it was time to visit the barbershop. He'd noticed a red-and-white-striped pole on one of the buildings near the saloon. A barbershop was a good place to obtain information.

Frank opened his saddlebags and retrieved the papers he had been collecting. Papers that chronicled all the crimes he was sure the Le Blanc gang had committed. Frank wanted to be sure they were in order when he took them to the sheriff.

As he shuffled through the pages he had collected, each one brought uncomfortable memories. If only the Old Man had been with Frank, he never would have insisted that Frank give up. Seeing all the devastation left behind by the Le Blancs, there was no way Frank could do that. As a lawman, he'd tried to protect people from evil people like Pierre Le Blanc. He couldn't allow other people to be destroyed by him, too.

Frank's hand stopped on the information from Cheyenne, Wyoming. He withdrew the slip of paper and moved to the window, reading the words in the glow from the gaslight and the moon. He didn't really need to see the words. He couldn't forget the stricken look on the face of a rancher who had been wiped out when his life savings were taken. Unfortunately, the man—like many others—didn't trust banking institutions. He'd hidden his savings under his mattress. That year had been hard, and the rancher was counting on that money to build up his depleted herd. He was even going to pay his hired hands with some of the cash.

Frank threw the paper down on the bed and stalked across the floor, rubbing the back of his neck. The man had lost heart along with his cash. When Frank left Cheyenne, the rancher was contemplating going back East to work in his brother's store—something he had declared he would never do.

Frank sat on the side of the bed and replaced the paper in the stack. He straightened the stack and started to slip it back into his saddlebag.

There was another face that Frank couldn't banish from his thoughts. A woman from Topeka, Kansas. The Le Blancs had taken jewelry from her—jewelry that had been in her family for over five generations. It had come from Europe with the ancestors who'd settled in Kansas while it was a wild land. When Frank met the woman, her eyes were red from weeping. She had shut herself off from most people, but the sheriff convinced her to talk to the marshal. She mourned the loss of the legacy she wanted to pass on to her daughters. While Frank questioned her, she showed him a portrait a traveling painter had done of her wearing some of the jewelry. They were beautiful pieces. Ever since then, he had been on the lookout for them in every town he passed through as he followed the trail of the Le Blanc gang.

Frank wondered what Le Blanc did with the jewelry and silver he stole. There wasn't much of a market for things like that in smaller towns. Perhaps he took it back East to sell. If so, Frank knew the owners would never see them again. It was a shame for a family to lose heirlooms like that.

While he undressed and got ready for bed, his thoughts returned to the graceful beauty. She was the kind of woman a man brought home to Mother, if his mother were still alive.

He didn't know that for a fact, but he thought he could tell that much about her. She walked with a regal bearing. The beauty would make a good mother for some man's children. Were the men in this town blind, or just stupid, to let a woman like her remain unmarried? Then another thought hit him. Was she a widow? Maybe she had been married. Perhaps there were children.

He could be mistaken about her. Maybe she was married but didn't wear a ring for some reason. But he couldn't dismiss the feeling that she was unattached. Frank had been good at reading people. He had to be in the business he was in.

Frank shook his head to clear it of the thoughts that haunted him. He crawled between clean sheets, which smelled like sunshine, and pulled up the colorful quilt that had been draped across the end of the bed. He was glad to be in a hotel that believed in cleanliness. He had slept plenty of times in beds with used sheets.

❧

Frank rode his horse, following Pierre Le Blanc and his two daughters, who were in a fancy buggy. They stayed just far enough ahead that he could barely make out their features, but he was sure it had to be them. They turned off the road and drove up to a farmhouse. A woman came out to meet them. She stood straight with glorious, light blond hair that was pulled up into a poufy hairstyle. He couldn't take his eyes off her. Her graceful hand waved toward him. He started to raise his but remembered what he had been doing when he saw her, so he didn't return her salute.

He glanced toward the Le Blancs, but they had disappeared. So had the buggy they were riding in. Nothing lay between him and the woman on the porch. He was no longer riding a horse, though he didn't remember dismounting. He strode across a grassy field toward the beauty who was now clothed in a creamy, shimmery dress that somehow looked familiar. The cool breeze blew the skirt out behind her, and the wisps of hair that fell around her shoulders also billowed in the wind. She smiled at him as if she were waiting for him.

"Welcome home."

Her melodious voice drifted on the spring breeze and caressed his ears. Her arms spread wide as if to emphasize the words, and he walked into her embrace. When her arms closed around him, she lifted her face to receive his kiss. He wanted to put his arms around her when he kissed her, but he couldn't move them. He struggled against the bonds that held him, but the more he struggled, the tighter they became.

Frank shook himself, and his eyes opened. He glanced around the unfamiliar place. In the light streaming through his window from the gaslight and a bright moon, he saw the flowered paper covering the walls above the wainscoting. Wind blew through the open window, and the curtains danced in the breeze. He glanced down. His body was trapped inside a cocoon of covers that wouldn't let him move. Frank snorted a derisive laugh. He must have been sleeping restlessly to become this entangled in his bedding.

Frank extricated himself from his bonds, got up, and walked to the window. Nothing moved outside, and the windows across the street were dark. He was probably the only person in town who was still awake.

The dream had seemed so real. He could almost smell the sweet woman who had thrown her arms around him and offered her lips for his kiss. He wished they had connected in the dream before he had awakened. Inner desires tormented him with things that could never happen.

three

Frank knew this night would be a long, sleepless one. It was quite awhile before dawn, but he dressed anyway. He stood at the window, leaning with both hands on the window frame, and studied the quiet street below. In the dream, the house had looked like his parents' old homestead when he was a boy, only with new paint. Often, his mother had waited on the porch and watched for his father the same way the woman in his dream had. In fact, when he first saw her standing there, she was wearing a dress much like the ones his mother wore. Perhaps the dream was trying to tell him something. Was he was ready to settle down and have a family similar to the happy family he grew up in?

The moon had moved across the sky while he slept, and its beams highlighted the dress in the window across the street. It shone like a pearl on black velvet, nestled against the darkness of the store's interior. Now he realized it was the dress the woman wore in his dream.

With a disgusted shake of his head, Frank turned toward the door. Maybe a walk in the cold night air would clear his head of the thoughts that plagued him. He needed to focus on the reason he came to this town. When he stepped out of the front door of the hotel, a nippy breeze caused gooseflesh to rise on his arms. He didn't care. Taking a cheroot from his pocket, Frank struck a match to light it. After taking several draws on it, he realized it didn't give him the satisfaction he usually felt when he smoked. He looked at the glowing tip before he flicked it into the dirt of the alley he was passing. He smashed it with the heel of his boot before continuing. His steps caused too much noise when he walked on the board-walk, so he stepped out into the street. Frank couldn't remem-ber when he had ever felt so restless. It was something more than just being near the object of his search. He couldn't put a name on the feeling, but he didn't like it at all. He was used to being completely in control of his emotions as well as his body.

The moon was three-quarters full, and it was sinking near the horizon. Frank glanced toward the east and could see the first, faint predawn light. He wondered how long it would be before the restaurant at the hotel would start serving breakfast. He went back into the lobby and up to his room to stretch out on his bed and wait until he smelled food cooking.

❧

When Gerda opened the Dress Emporium the next morn-ing, Clarissa Jenson was her first customer. Gerda was glad that someone had come to the shop so early. It would help take her thoughts off the man who had invaded her dreams. Although they hadn't made any sense, his presence was over-whelming, clouding her mind.

"Clari!" Gerda and Anna had picked up the habit of call-ing the twin sisters by the shortened names they used for each other. "What brings you out so early in the morning?"

Clarissa gave Gerda a quick hug. "Ollie and I have the house fixed up the way we want it. It's a good thing, too." A dreamy expression covered Clarissa's face like a veil. "Soon there will be something else to take all my attention."

"You don't mean. . . ?" Gerda wondered if this couple was going to have a child before her brother August and his wife, Anna, would. The Nilssons had been married longer, and they wanted a child so much.

Clarissa nodded. "We're going to have a baby. So I need you to make me some clothes to wear while I'm expanding."

"I'm so happy for you." Gerda hugged Clarissa again. "You've had too many bad things happen in your life. I'm glad that has changed."

Clarissa stepped back and rubbed her hands down her skirt. "The good things started several months ago when Pierre was sent to prison—and when God brought Ollie into my life."

She went over to the counter where several fashion books were arranged and started leafing through one. "Do you have any ideas about what I'll need?"

"I always enjoy creating lovely clothing to help women hide their growing figures while they wait for the birth of their child." Gerda must have sounded wistful, because Clarissa looked concerned. Gerda didn't want her to think she was unhappy. "Why don't we go to the ice cream parlor to celebrate when we've finished choosing styles and materials?"

Clarissa walked to the display of fabrics on the shelves behind the counter and started running her fingers over different pieces, feeling their textures. "Actually, Mari and I are meeting there at ten o'clock, but you could join us. I'm afraid I've been craving one of those chocolate sundaes." She patted her flat stomach for emphasis. "Having a baby makes a woman want strange things sometimes. A couple of days ago, I mentioned to Ollie that I would really like one of the pickles from the barrel in the mercantile, and he came to town and bought some."

It took until almost ten o'clock for Clarissa to make up her mind about what fabrics to use for her new outfits. Gerda couldn't help remembering how concerned she and Anna had been when Rissa Le Blanc kept changing her mind about the colors and styles of the dresses they were making for her. How surprised they had been to find out that there was no Rissa Le Blanc! Instead, the twins were playing a part their stepfather had created. Finally, the two dressmakers understood. Although the twins looked a lot alike, their tastes were very different. Their styles fit their personalities. Clarissa was more outgoing, and Marissa was the quieter sister. And Gerda loved both of them.

※

Frank fell into a deep, dreamless sleep just before dawn. When he finally awoke, he cleaned up and shaved before he went to the dining room to see if he could get a late breakfast. Some places served all day, and others only at mealtime. He hoped this restaurant was one that didn't have specific hours.

Molly, who had waited on him the night before, met him at the door. "How can we help you, Mr. Daggett?"

"Molly, I'm afraid I overslept." He smiled at the older woman. "Do you think I could still get some breakfast?"

"Let me go ask Cook. I know she has started on lunch, but maybe she can do something for you. If not, I can make you some toast."

She headed toward the kitchen, and Frank sat down at a table near the window. He didn't think he could make it until lunch on only a couple pieces of toast, even if he loaded them with butter and jelly. A newspaper was lying on the table, so he picked it up and perused it until she returned.

"It just so happens that there is still some flapjack batter left. How does that sound?" A smile accompanied the waitress's question.

When Frank agreed, she returned to the kitchen. Before long, she came back, but she didn't have just buckwheat flapjacks with a tin of maple syrup. The cook was kind enough to make him bacon and eggs, too. He left the hotel fortified for a full day's activities.

The sun was high in the sky when he stepped onto the boardwalk. He pulled the brim of his Stetson low to shade his eyes from the glare off the windows across the street.

Frank glanced down toward the saloon. All seemed to be quiet on that end of town. When he looked across the street, he was astonished to see Rissa Le Blanc exiting that dress shop he had noticed the night before. It had to be her. She looked exactly like the drawing one of their victims had made of her. He was right. Pierre and the other girl, if there was another girl, must be nearby. Here in Litchfield, Minnesota. When Frank had first headed this direction, he had been afraid it was too far north for this Southern family. His gut instincts kept urging him on. And he had learned long ago to trust his instincts.

Frank had even started to wonder if he had lost his touch, but since they were here, now he knew he hadn't. All he had to do was keep an eye on this girl and let her lead him to Pierre. He wanted to catch that villain and make him and his accomplices pay for all the crimes they had committed.

Trying to act nonchalant, Frank sidled down the board-walk in the direction the girl took. He kept his head down, so she wouldn't notice that he was watching her from under the brim of his hat. Soon the Le Blanc woman went into the ice cream parlor. He continued walking toward the store. When he reached it, he leaned against the wall and pulled his knife and a small block of wood from his pocket. While he whittled on the wood, he could keep up with what was going on inside.

After he took a few small shavings from the wood, he studied the ice cream parlor from the corners of his eyes.

Rissa Le Blanc sat at a table near some planters that looked remarkably like brass spittoons. She looked at the door as if she were waiting for someone. Maybe Le Blanc. Frank's senses sharpened and his blood pumped through his veins at an accelerated rate. He took a deep breath and exhaled. He could almost smell victory.

❧

From the doorway of the Dress Emporium, Gerda watched Clarissa walk across the street toward the ice cream parlor. When she started to turn back into the store, she saw the cowboy head up the street. He seemed to be watching Clari. Of course, she couldn't blame him. Clarissa was a very beautiful woman. When Clari went into the ice cream parlor, he sauntered toward it as if he were following her. He didn't look eager, as he might if he wanted to flirt with her. It was more like he was stalking her. Gerda got a funny feeling deep inside. Something wasn't quite right. She felt that Clarissa was in danger or. . .something. Maybe he was someone from Clarissa's past, someone who had been swindled. Gerda didn't think he was a lawman. Didn't they usually wear badges? He wasn't wearing one, although he did look more like a cowboy than he had at dinner last night. She could hear his spurs jingling as he walked down the boardwalk.

When he stopped and leaned against the building outside the ice cream parlor, she studied him intently. She wasn't sure, but she thought he was watching Clarissa, even though he looked like he was whittling. He looked as if he were a spring that was wound really tight.

She stepped back inside and rushed into the back room for her wool cape and her reticule, then went out the front door, trying to appear nonchalant. Gerda locked the door to the Dress Emporium and hurried across the railroad tracks toward

August's blacksmith shop. He would know what to do to protect Clarissa and Marissa.

&

When he noticed the beauty exiting the dress shop, Frank was distracted from both watching the Le Blanc girl and whittling. The woman turned and locked the front door of the store. *She must be the proprietor. No wonder the dress in the window would look good on her. She probably created it.*

The image of a woman pulling down the window shade above the dress shop returned to Frank's mind. It was probably her. Now that he thought about it, the bit of skirt he had seen did resemble what she'd worn at dinner last night. He had watched her long enough that he should have recognized it when he saw it later. He just wasn't thinking of her being there, so it hadn't occurred to him. Again, Frank wondered if anyone else lived there with her—like a husband or children.

When the woman swept down the street and past the depot, he wondered where she was going in such a hurry. He glanced back into the confectionary shop. Rissa Le Blanc still sat at a table by herself. He started whittling again. Someday, he needed to learn how to really make something when he whittled. For now, it was merely a ploy he used in order to appear busy when he was tailing someone. No one knew he just chipped small pieces off the block of wood until it was as small as a toothpick. Then he'd throw it away and start on another block.

He'd gotten the idea from watching his grandfather whittle, when he was a small boy. The things that emerged from the blocks of wood Gramps worked on were wondrous. The toy soldiers, small animals, even sailing ships his grandfather had whittled had given Frank hours of enjoyment as a child. It was too bad he had never learned the craft from Gramps.

❧

It was still a cool spring, but before Gerda arrived at the black-smith shop, she wished she had left off the wool cape that matched her dress. She hurried, because she didn't want to be too late meeting with Marissa and Clarissa. By the time she arrived at the open door of the smithy, she was almost out of breath. Her shadow must have alerted her brother to her presence, because he turned from what he was doing.

"Gerda, come in." A smile spread across August's face. "What can I do for you? Do you have something for me to fix?"

She put her hand to her throat and took a deep breath. "No, I don't need anything repaired. But I do need your help. I don't know what to do!"

August rushed over to her and looked deep into her eyes. "What has upset you?"

"Well, I don't know if it's anything or not." Her words tumbled out in rapid succession. "But that cowboy is following Clari, and I don't want anything to happen to her. Especially now that she's going to have a baby."

August looked confused. "Slow down, sister. You're talking too fast. Now what cowboy?"

Gerda pulled off the cape and draped it over her arm. "Well, there's this cowboy. He's new in town. He was at the hotel last night when we had dinner."

August nodded. "I saw him, but I didn't pay that much attention to him. Why do you think he's following Clarissa?"

Suddenly, Gerda wondered if she had made too much out of what she'd seen. He could just be a drifter. Maybe he just happened to walk down the street after Clarissa did. It could all be merely a coincidence. What if she was mistaken? Deep inside, the worry wouldn't go away.

"He watched Clarissa go to the ice cream parlor. Then he followed her but stopped and leaned against the outside wall and started whittling. Then I got this uncomfortable feeling about it. I just don't want anything bad to happen to Clarissa or Marissa. They're meeting there for a treat."

August put his arm around her shoulders. "I've learned to trust women's intuition. Even if there isn't anything wrong, I'll go check it out." He went to the table and took off his apron. Then he banked the fire in the forge. He turned toward the door. "You go back to the store, and I'll take care of it."

Gerda shook her head. "I can't. I'm supposed to meet Clari and Mari at the ice cream parlor. We're going to celebrate together."

August laughed. "Oh, yes, you did mention something about a baby, didn't you?"

"Yes, she and Ollie are expecting. You don't think it'll make Anna feel bad, do you?"

"Don't worry about that." He closed the door and dropped the board into the holders. "She'll be happy for them. Our time will come. You go ahead, and I'll follow at a slower pace. I don't want the man to know we're together. Just be careful."

four

While Frank watched the beauty walking rapidly down the road, he mechanically continued to work on the block of wood with his knife. He liked the way her hips swayed with each quick step. If only his life wasn't so complicated. He shook his head. The woman surely was a temptation to him. Suddenly, he felt the tip of the sharp blade nick his finger. The words that came to mind weren't suitable for mixed company, and there was more than one woman in his vicinity, so he kept them to himself. He looked down in time to see a large drop of blood leave his finger and make its way to the toe of his boot. He quickly closed his pocketknife with his other hand and shoved both it and the block of wood into his pocket.

Frank didn't want to leave his post, but he needed to take care of the wound he had carelessly inflicted on himself. How could he have been so stupid? He knew better than to let his mind wander. His finger was bleeding pretty fast now. He pulled out his bandanna and wrapped it around his fingertip. After glancing in the window of the ice cream parlor to make sure Rissa was still there, Frank started toward the hotel. She was sitting at the table and looked as if she were waiting for someone. Maybe Le Blanc would be here soon. But they couldn't know that he was looking for them. He should be able to make it to his hotel room and back before they were ready to leave the store.

While he was in his hotel room, he called himself all kinds

of unflattering names for the harebrained stunt he had pulled. The tip of his finger was awkward to bandage, and now the digit throbbed enough to make him extremely uncomfortable. He might have a hard time pulling his gun with it, but at least it was his left hand. If he needed to use his guns quickly, he might only have one good trigger finger, but it should be enough. His aim was always on target. In his business, you often only had one chance before someone else shot you.

Frank glanced toward the ice cream parlor when he exited the hotel. Another girl, who looked remarkably like the one sitting at the table, was just going through the door. Only this young woman had on a different dress. Her hair was in a more simple style, too. He was right. How he wished the Old Man could see them. He'd change his tune now. There *were* two girls, and they were in that building together! Frank paused. Something didn't feel right. He had never heard of both of the young women showing themselves at the same time. He'd have to be careful. Maybe Litchfield was their base of operations and everyone here knew both of the young women. Maybe their neighbors didn't know what they did for a living.

He took up his post against the ice cream parlor, but this time, Frank had left the block of wood in his hotel room. He started to pull out a cheroot. However, he didn't want to be smoking when they exited the shop. Frank reached up and pulled the brim of his Stetson lower.

Before his hand reached his headgear, the beauty from the Dress Emporium walked past him. She looked him straight in the eye. The disdain in her expression cut him just as much as the knife blade had cut his finger—maybe even more. Why did he care what she thought of him? She was just a pretty woman he had enjoyed watching. Nothing more. Right?

&

When Gerda first glanced toward the ice cream parlor, the cowboy was gone. She had probably bothered August for nothing. She wondered if she should go back and tell him. But she wasn't exactly sure where he was right now. She slowed down after she crossed the railroad tracks. It wouldn't look ladylike for her to rush down the street.

When the stranger emerged from the hotel and started down the street, she hoped he was going somewhere else. By the time she arrived at the ice cream parlor, he had taken up his post again, leaning against the wall. She gave him her most withering expression as she passed. Maybe he would take the hint and leave. Unfortunately, he just stared back at her, but his expression was unfathomable. If only his eyes weren't so blue. Each time she looked into them, they touched a place deep inside, piercing through all her defenses. Even though she suspected the cowboy of stalking Clarissa, Gerda felt drawn to him as she had never felt with any man before.

Gerda really wanted to enjoy her time with her friends, but it would be hard to forget that the cowboy was just outside the building. All the worries she harbored about him returned. . .and brought a few friends with them.

"Gerda." Clarissa smiled up at her when she stopped by the table where they sat. "I was about to think you weren't coming."

"I'm sorry I kept you waiting." Gerda pulled out at chair and sat with them. "What shall we order?" She always felt as if she were sitting in a park every time she came to the ice cream parlor. The flowers on the mural painted around the wall were so realistic she could almost smell them.

The friends discussed all the offerings, then Gerda went to the counter to order a phosphate for herself and ice cream sundaes for both Marissa and Clarissa. Gerda had to wait behind a woman and young child who were having a hard time deciding what they wanted. After ordering, Gerda returned to the table where Clarissa and Marissa sat talking.

While they waited for the treats to be concocted, Marissa blurted, "I have a surprise to tell you." Both young women leaned forward, eager to hear. "I've just been to see Dr. Bradley."

"Oh, Mari, are you sick?" Clarissa exclaimed. She reached across the table and took her sister's hand.

"I hope not." Gerda cared about the twins as though they were her sisters.

"It's nothing like that." Marissa smiled and glanced down before raising her head again.

Clarissa looked worried. "Then why did you go to the doctor? Is something wrong with Lowell or Mother Jenson?"

Marissa laughed. "I can't keep the secret any longer. Lowell and I are going to have a baby."

For a moment they all talked at once, so no one could understand what anyone was saying. The proprietor brought their treats on a tray and set them on the table.

Marissa tasted the sundae, then looked from Gerda to Clarissa. "I am so happy. Both Lowell and I want lots of children. When I told him that I thought I might be expecting a baby, he wanted me to come right to town and have the doctor check. So I can't stay too long. He'll want to know what I found out."

"Mari, this is so wonderful!" Clarissa clapped her hands. She glanced at Gerda, then at her sister. "I'm going to have a baby, too! I found out for sure yesterday. Ollie is so proud, his chest puffed out like a peacock's."

Marissa's smile broadened more. "Oh, Clari, I'm so glad!"

Gerda watched the twins share a special look. They often did that, but today the look was different. Gerda knew it was because they were both expecting a child. Would she never get to share that feeling? Why was God denying her a husband and children when they were her heart's desire?

"Do you girls always do the same thing at the same time? Your husbands proposed to you on the same day. You had double weddings, and now you're both going to have a baby."

"It'll be wonderful for our babies to each have a cousin almost the same age." Clarissa reached across the table and took her sister's hand again.

"And one that lives so close, too," Marissa added, returning the strong grip.

The sisters started giggling. Soon Gerda joined them. Even with her disappointment, she was happy for her friends. Out of the corner of her eye, she could see that the young worker behind the counter was smiling at them. Soon the word would be all over town that everyone was having babies. Of course, in a town like Litchfield, it was hard to keep secrets.

The man standing outside the building came into Gerda's thoughts. She knew he was hiding something. She hoped that soon his secret would be revealed, too. Then the man could move on, and her thoughts would return to normal. Wouldn't they?

༄

Frank couldn't believe it. Not only did the beauty go into the ice cream parlor, she sat at the table with the Le Blanc sisters. They were obviously close friends. Could she be in cahoots with them? Was she part of the gang? He didn't want to entertain that thought, but it wouldn't let him go. Time would tell.

Was Le Blanc coming to join them? While Frank kept watch on the women in the shop, he also scanned the street looking for the confidence man who had hoodwinked so many people across the country. The man was a menace to society. Le Blanc insinuated himself into a community, making the citizens think that he was someone important. He flashed money around and hosted parties until everyone he considered special in that town knew him. Then Le Blanc pulled a fast one on his victims. Now Frank knew how he had accomplished it. Exactly the way Frank had figured it out a few months earlier. Today was the first time he had evidence that his theory was correct.

Le Blanc only let the people in town meet one of his daughters. Then during some kind of community event, the other daughter robbed many of the people who were in attendance. If anyone saw her, Le Blanc had proof that his daughter was with him at the event. He soon left town, and no one was sure who had committed the robberies. In some of the towns, the sheriff was still looking for another perpetrator of the crimes.

Frank wondered which of the young women at the table was actually Rissa. What was the other woman's name? Did both of them participate in the crimes, or only one? He hoped he would find out when he took them into custody later today.

The only fly in the ointment was the presence of the other woman—the beauty. Last night he had been so sure that she was a decent, upright citizen. How could he have been so wrong? Was she Le Blanc's mistress or accomplice. . .or just his friend? If she was a proprietor here in Litchfield, how did she fit in the picture of the other places where Le Blanc had been? Or was she just a new acquaintance of the gang? He sure hoped so. It was going to hurt him to have to take her into custody. But a lawman always did his duty, even when it hurt. And no matter if the Old Man had made him turn in his badge, he was still a lawman at heart.

Frank glanced up and down the street again. He had watched several people go in, then come out of the mercantile carrying packages wrapped in brown paper. Several people came and went at the bank. Wagons and men on horseback traveled up and down the street at frequent intervals. When Frank had first seen Litchfield on the horizon, it had looked like a sleepy town, but he had been wrong about that. It was a thriving, vital town. It seemed like a nice place to live and bring up a family. That woman in the ice cream parlor was affecting him. He hadn't had so many thoughts about a family in a long time.

If Le Blanc were going to join the women, Frank wished the scoundrel would do it soon. Frank was getting tired of standing in this spot. He peeked into the window. The young women were busy talking. It didn't look as if they would be ready to leave any time soon. Frank decided to stroll up and down the street. He could look into the windows of other businesses to see if he could spot Le Blanc. Maybe by the time he got back here, the women would be finished visiting. He would keep a sharp eye on the place and not get too far away, in case they came out.

᠉

Gerda saw the cowboy when he walked past the front of the store. It was all she could do to keep from shouting, she was so glad to see him go. Perhaps it was just a coincidence that he came along when he did. He just happened to choose to lean against this building. That's all.

"What do you think, Gerda?" Clarissa's words brought Gerda's attention back to the conversation at the table.

"About what? I'm afraid I was distracted."

Clarissa looked toward the window. "What distracted you, Gerda? Was it that cowboy walking down the street?"

Gerda hoped she wasn't that obvious. "Of course not." After a good laugh, she asked what they had been talking about.

"Marissa wants you to make her some clothes, too. Will you have time to do both?"

"It would be my pleasure. Besides, Anna still comes in to work a couple of days a week. She has her hands full keeping up that big house, and she helps Olina with the children sometimes."

"Let's go back to the Dress Emporium so Marissa can pick out her fabrics and styles," said Clarissa. Gerda stood and glanced across the shop toward the now-empty counter.

"I'm going to pay for our treats. Just wait for me."

When she got back to the table, both of the sisters were standing. As they trio stepped out into the sunlight, their eyes had to adjust to the brightness.

"Just hold it right there!" The rich baritone voice came from behind Gerda, and expressions of horror covered Marissa's and Clarissa's faces as they stared over her shoulder.

Gerda turned to see what was going on and came face-to-face with the cowboy. The man had both of his six-shooters trained on the women!

five

Frank watched the three women finish their treats. When they seemed ready to leave the building, he pulled his hat lower on his forehead and turned to wait for them. His body was wound tight as an eight-day clock as he watched them glide toward the door as though they were walking on clouds. His hands hovered near his pistols while he tried to figure out how to handle the next few minutes. He hadn't seen the sheriff or Le Blanc, and now that he was so close, he worried that the women were about to slip away from him. How was he ever going to keep up with three women? If they split up, which one should he follow? Which one would lead him to Le Blanc? Before he could decide, the women were at the entrance. Making a lightning-quick decision, he pulled his guns. It would be better to have the three women in custody than to let any of them get away to warn Pierre. Maybe Le Blanc would come out of hiding to rescue them. Frank hoped so. The women stepped outside and froze with shocked expressions on their faces.

"Just hold it right there!" Frank bit out. "You're all under arrest."

The beauty was the first to react. "Arrest!" she screamed as she whirled toward him. Frank was surprised at the volume of her shriek. "You can't arrest us! We're not criminals! Besides, you aren't a lawman!"

Frank didn't know what kind of reaction he had expected, but it wasn't this. Why couldn't they just come quietly? He didn't want to create a disturbance. He planned to simply apprehend them, take them to the sheriff, then slip out of town. There was no need for anyone besides the sheriff and the Le Blanc gang to even know why he was here—or that he wasn't a real lawman anymore. Because he didn't want any of them to get away, Frank didn't dare look to see if anyone else in the street had noticed the hullabaloo.

"I'm a retired U.S. Marshal, and I'm taking you to the sheriff." Frank tried to keep his voice low, but authoritative.

"We'll go to the sheriff with you," the beauty said just as quietly, then took a deep breath as if fortifying herself. "He'll straighten this all out."

Suddenly, a strong arm snaked around Frank's neck, almost choking him. Who could it be, and how did the man get there without making any noise on the boardwalk?

The man holding him was much larger than, and too strong to be, Le Blanc. Muscles bulged as the man's arm tightened around Frank's neck. Quickly, Frank holstered one gun and fought to pull the arm from around his neck so he could breathe easier. It tightened even more. Breathing was becoming more difficult for Frank. Black spots danced before his eyes, and he dropped the other gun. He heard it bounce off the boardwalk and hit the dirt street.

A deep voice sounded from over his shoulder. "Gerda, take the gun from his holster, and I'll let him go."

Frank hoped she would hurry. He didn't want to pass out right here in the middle of town. Just as he was about to lose consciousness, he felt the gun being lifted away. The arm around his neck loosened slightly, and his vision cleared in time to see the beauty raising the pistol, which she then pointed straight at him.

Frank was glad no one he knew lived in this town. He would never be able to live down the fact that he'd let a criminal, a female one at that, get the drop on him.

When August told her to get the gun, Gerda straightened her spine and stood taller. She didn't have to be afraid of the man while August held him. She reached over and took the weapon gingerly. When she felt its weight in her hand, something happened. It gave her a sense of power. She lifted the barrel and turned it toward the cowboy. *Let's see how you like having a gun pointed at you.* She glanced at August and nodded.

"All right, Cowboy, I'm going to let you go, but don't make any sudden movements or Gerda will shoot you."

Gerda couldn't believe what August said. She would never shoot anyone. And even though she knew she shouldn't, Gerda felt something for this cowboy. She wasn't sure what it was, but she couldn't shoot him, even if he did make a sudden move. Whatever she felt for him, it made her uncomfortable. A vision of the barrel of a gun pointed at her temple returned, and something inside her snapped.

"How could you?" She waved the barrel of the gun toward him. "What were you trying to do with these guns? Kill innocent women?" The look on the man's face would have been comical to Gerda if she hadn't been so angry. "I can't believe I felt so drawn to you when I first saw you. You're nothing but a common criminal yourself."

Gerda glanced from the gun in her hand toward the man's face. The expression in his eyes reached out to her, and she burst into tears. Clarissa grabbed the gun from Gerda and turned it back toward the cowboy. August pulled the man's hands behind his back and held them with one giant hand. He turned the cowboy toward the sheriff's office, and they started walking.

Marissa pulled a handkerchief from her reticule and gave it to Gerda. Then she patted her friend on the back. Gerda was mortified. People were staring. Some were whispering among themselves. She didn't think she would ever live this down. Marissa took her arm, and they followed the others toward the sheriff's office.

Sheriff Bartlett must have heard the disturbance, because he was running toward them.

≈

Frank didn't know when he had ever been so glad to see a sheriff. Now the man would rescue him from this gang. But something wasn't quite right. If they were criminals, why did the strong man want to take him to the sheriff—unless he was part of the gang, too? *Maybe the whole town is in on this with the Le Blancs. Stay calm, Frank. Don't lose your edge.*

When they were all inside the small office, the sheriff offered his only two chairs to the Le Blanc sisters. "I'm sorry I don't have another chair, Gerda." He smiled at the beauty, and Frank didn't like the way it made him feel.

Gerda. Frank liked the sound of her name. It fit her Scandinavian good looks.

"It's all right." She paced across the small space. "I'm too upset to sit down."

The burly man who had grabbed Frank in front of the ice cream parlor put his arm around Gerda. Frank didn't like that either. Was this woman some kind of doxy? How could she seem so pure and untouched if she was that kind of woman?

"Calm down, Sis." The big man's words were a balm to Frank's troubled heart. She was the man's sister. But that didn't clear up anything. They could still both be part of the Le Blanc gang.

The sheriff took Frank's gun from the Le Blanc girl. He laid it on his desk. At least it was no longer pointed at Frank.

"Now who's going to tell me what's going on?" The sheriff held up one hand. "And I want to hear one person at a time.

Clarissa Jenson, since you were holding the gun on this man, why don't you start?"

Jenson. Her name was Jenson, not Le Blanc. Frank's jumbled thoughts kept him from hearing all the woman said.

"And he was pointing his guns at us," she finished.

"Where is his other gun?" The sheriff looked at each person in turn.

The other twin, who seemed more reserved, spoke up. "I have it. When August grabbed him, it fell into the street, so I picked it up. . .in case we needed it, too. I didn't like touching it, so I put it in my reticule to carry it over here."

"Mari, you hate guns!" The Jenson woman looked at her sister with a worried expression on her face.

"I know, but I couldn't let him hurt Gerda or August."

The woman was trembling like a maple leaf in the breeze. She pulled the gun from her handbag and, holding it between her thumb and forefinger, gave it to the sheriff. He placed it beside the one on his desk.

"Thank you, Marissa." The lawman looked at Frank. "All right. Who are you, and why are you bothering these fine folks?"

Frank stared the man straight in his eyes. They weren't shifty. The corrupt lawmen he had known before wouldn't look him in the eyes. This man did. Maybe he was honest. Frank had to take that chance.

"Frank Daggett, former U.S. Marshal. I've been on the trail of a gang of robbers who have carried out confidence games in many states. I have documents detailing their crimes which I intended to deliver to you once I had placed the gang in your custody." He stopped at the irony—it had turned out a little different than he'd anticipated.

Frank looked at the sisters as he gestured toward them. He was sure they would be cowering in their chairs. Instead, they were smiling. Maybe he had made a mistake. His glance shot back to the sheriff, and he was smiling, too. A sense of doom settled over Frank. Why hadn't he stopped when the Old Man told him to?

He heard a burst of laughter. The brother and sister were almost doubled over with mirth. The sheriff's guffaw joined theirs.

When Frank turned to look at him, the lawman was holding Frank's guns out to him. "You might as well take these, since you're not a criminal."

Frank returned his weapons to their holsters, then asked, "Is anyone going to let me in on what's so amusing here?"

The sheriff sat on the corner of his desk. "You drew your guns on these three women because you thought they were criminals. Right?"

Frank nodded.

When he did, Gerda glared at him. "You thought *I* was a criminal?" She placed her fisted hands on her waist, with her arms akimbo.

He nodded again, unable to voice the answer to the question.

"I've never been so insulted in my life." She whirled around and started toward the door.

Her brother followed her, and the sheriff turned toward the twin sisters. "I wouldn't want Lowell and Ollie to think you were in trouble. You can go, too. I'll explain everything to Mr. Daggett."

The door closed behind them, and the sheriff looked at Frank. "This is really something! You're about," he said as he counted on his fingers, "eight months too late."

Frank felt as if he had stepped into the middle of a discussion and had been asked a question about what had gone on before. "I don't understand. Eight months too late for what?"

"Maybe you should sit down while I tell you all about it."

The sheriff motioned toward the chair that had recently been vacated by one of the twins. "Actually, I admire your tenacity—to follow Le Blanc's trail so faithfully."

Frank ducked his head and rubbed the back of his neck. Tenacity. That's what he had all right. The Old Man had often told him that he was like an old dog with a bone.

"Pierre Le Blanc is a very evil man." The sheriff propped his booted feet on the corner of his desk and leaned back in his chair. "He planned to rob the good folks of Litchfield, just as you figured."

"What stopped him?"

"Well, it was a lot of things. People in this town had become fond of Rissa Le Blanc—especially the Nilsson family." The sheriff dropped his feet back on the floor and leaned forward as if eager to get on with the story. "None of us knew that there were two girls, and neither one of them was really Rissa Le Blanc. Pierre, their stepfather, called whichever one was in town with him 'Rissa.' It was part of each of their names. Clarissa and Marissa. Is this getting too confusing for you?"

Frank leaned his forearms on his thighs. "I had pretty much decided there had to be two girls. That was the only way he could get away with all he did."

The sheriff chuckled. "The man was clever. I'll give him that. He kept one girl in a camp quite a ways from town in an area where not many people ventured. He planned to rob the town while most everyone was at the circus. It was the first time the circus had ever come here, so it was a good plan."

Frank's interest was piqued. "Then what went wrong with his plan?"

"This is where it gets complicated." The sheriff laughed. "Both of the Jenson brothers had a hankering for Rissa Le Blanc. It caused a lot of friction between them."

"I can understand that. They're good-looking women."

Frank sat back in the chair and propped one foot on the other knee.

"Lowell is the quieter brother. He decided to go camping to think about things and he stumbled across their camp. Le Blanc had left both girls there, which they later said was unusual. Lowell went back to the farm to get his brother. When they returned, they learned about Le Blanc's scheme and convinced the girls to help us catch Pierre in the act."

"That could have been dangerous, couldn't it?"

"Yes, but the girls felt as if they were their stepfather's prisoners. It was a way for them to finally be free of him." The sheriff stood up. "So that's why you are eight months too late. That's when we had the trial that put Le Blanc in prison for life."

Frank stood up, too. "What can you tell me about the Nilssons?"

"That's another interesting family. Good folks. They came from Sweden, originally." The sheriff sat on the front corner of his desk. "There are three brothers and one sister. Gustaf works the farm with his dad, August is the blacksmith in town, and Lars moved to Denver. Gerda is part owner of the Dress Emporium. She lives in an apartment above the store."

The door burst open, and Hank, the owner of the livery stable, came in. "Sheriff, I need to talk to you." He stopped short when he noticed Frank. "Sorry, I didn't mean to interrupt."

"That's all right." Frank picked up his hat from the floor beside where he had been sitting. "I was just going." He turned toward the sheriff. "I'll buy you coffee sometime, Sheriff."

When Frank arrived at the hotel, everyone in the lobby looked at him as he headed toward the stairs at the back of the room. Just what he needed. Everyone in town would talk about him until something happened to take their minds off what he'd done. He hoped that event would come soon. Of course, Frank could leave town now. The Old Man might give him his badge back. Probably, the Old Man already knew about Le Blanc being in prison and was expecting Frank to come back. But he didn't want to leave town without trying to get to know Gerda Nilsson. Frank wondered why no man had claimed her for his own. She seemed to be beautiful through and through. How could he have ever thought Gerda was a fallen woman? He was going to have to make that thought up to her somehow.

Frank paused with his boot resting on the bottom step. He glanced at the desk clerk. Just as Frank suspected, the man was watching him. When Frank looked at him, he quickly averted his gaze to something behind the counter.

After raking his fingers down his bristly cheek, Frank decided that what he needed most was a bath and shave. "Would you have hot water sent up to my room?"

The desk clerk glanced up at him. "Yes, sir."

Frank continued up the carpeted staircase. It was a good thing the Jenson brothers found the campsite and rescued the sisters from Le Blanc's clutches. It was a shame that their stepfather had been able to hold them in servitude. The sheriff had assured Frank that even though it had gone on so many years, the young women hadn't become corrupted. If Frank believed in a God, he would have been sure that God had protected them all that time. But Frank had never been able to believe that a loving God would allow all the bad things he'd seen in his lifetime. He could remember his mother and grandmother praying for him when he was a little boy, but when he left home, he put all that behind him.

After he had scraped the whiskers from his cheeks, he gathered up his clothes and went down the hall to the bathroom. At least this hotel had all the modern amenities. Some of the places Frank had stayed didn't. In those places, the proprietor hauled up a large galvanized tub and lots of hot water for a person to take a bath in the bedroom.

Frank immersed himself in the warm water and began to lather his arms with the lye soap. It would have been nice to have something a little kinder to his skin. Maybe he would go to the mercantile and see what they had for sale. He could buy something better to use. That was a good excuse to go to the store. What reason could he use to go into the Dress Emporium? He had never been to a circus. Maybe he could ask Gerda about it.

⁂

Gerda swept through the door of the sheriff's office, glad that August accompanied her. Out on the street, everyone stared at the two of them while they walked to the Dress Emporium. She was tempted to keep the store closed. She didn't want anyone coming in asking questions. Wasn't it enough that they were the spectacle of the day?

However, Clarissa and Marissa were coming to choose patterns and fabrics for Marissa's new clothing. Gerda couldn't turn them away.

If she could only keep from thinking about that cowboy— that former U.S. Marshal. The gall of the man, thinking she was a criminal! How could she have ever been drawn to him? God surely had a man in mind for her, and he wouldn't be someone who could think something like that about her. Gerda hoped she would never see the man again. Maybe he would leave town as soon as he knew the whole story. It couldn't be soon enough for her.

six

When Frank finished bathing and dressing, he went to Braxton's Mercantile. He was pleasantly surprised to see all the merchandise the store had to offer. He had been in a lot of businesses scattered all across the country. This establishment would compare favorably with many in large cities like Chicago. He hadn't thought he would find such an assortment of high-quality goods tucked away here in the heart of Minnesota. Frank browsed through the sundries and picked up some scented coal tar soap. He held the paper wrapping to his nose to check the fragrance. It had a nice, masculine aroma, and coal tar soap was easy on the skin. Sitting on the shelf alongside the bath soap was an assortment of shaving bars and brushes. The brush he had been using was wearing out, so he chose one with bristles that didn't seem too soft or too stiff. Since no one else was nearby, he tested it by swirling it against his cheek. It felt good, so he added it and two bars of shaving soap to the things he was carrying and headed toward the counter at the back of the store.

At that point, Frank realized that several other people were shopping in the large establishment. He could feel their eyes trained on him. He didn't want to turn around and see if they were talking about him. The walk toward the man at the counter was uncomfortable. Frank didn't like to be the center of attention, and he wondered why he hadn't just stayed in his hotel room until everyone forgot what happened.

Frank had been talked about before, but he didn't like it.

He held his head a little higher and continued down an aisle between shelves containing an assortment of men's clothing. Perhaps it was time to replenish his wardrobe. He'd kept his possessions to a minimum while he was on the trail of the gang. How long had it been now? Frank didn't want to think about the number of years that he had wasted chasing a phantom.

He would have to make some decision soon about what to do now. He could go and ask the Old Man for his job back, but Frank wasn't sure that was what he wanted to do. When the talk died down, Litchfield, Minnesota, might be the place for him to settle into a normal life. If it wasn't too late for that. And gnawing at the back of his mind were the words Gerda had blurted when she was holding the gun on him. She'd felt the same strong sense of connection he had that first time he laid eyes on her in the hotel lobby.

When he reached the counter, the man behind it smiled at him. *That's a good sign.* Frank decided to act as if nothing out of the ordinary had happened.

"I'm Frank Daggett." He set the soaps and brush on the wooden structure. The man with sandy red hair and lots of freckles had blue eyes that sparkled with friendliness.

"Glad to meet you, Mr. Daggett. I'm Claude Dawson." He reached for the merchandise Frank had laid on the counter.

"This is a real nice store you have here, Mr. Dawson." Frank turned and perused the rest of the refreshingly clean establishment while he leaned on the counter with one arm.

"Oh, I'm not the proprietor." The clerk shook his head. "I work for the Braxtons. Please call me Claude."

Frank straightened away from the counter and smiled back. "All right, Claude. If someone wanted to settle in Litchfield, what is there to do here?"

Claude looked him up and down as if assessing his attributes. "Well, I'm just working to make enough money to move to California. I almost have enough saved, so you could take my place here. Or there are a couple of businesses for sale. What have you done before?"

Frank decided that maybe the sheriff was a closemouthed man if word of what happened hadn't even reached the clerk in the store. "I've been in law enforcement, but I want to settle down. I like the looks of the town."

"Claude, did you receive my shipment from Boston?" The feminine voice sounded from across the room, but it was coming closer. "I need it as soon as. . ."

As the melodious words stopped abruptly, Frank turned and smiled. "Hello, Gerda."

ia.

When had that lawman come into the store? Gerda felt flustered. She probably hadn't recognized him because he had cleaned up since their infamous encounter earlier that morning. She couldn't keep from staring into his blue eyes. The clear, icy color had turned warm in a way she hadn't anticipated. She wanted to look away, but she couldn't tear her gaze from his eyes. *Animal magnetism.* That's what that man had. Where had she heard that term? Probably in one of those dime novels she had been reading since Anna had moved out of the apartment. The man's body was sleek, like a cougar, all sinews and strength.

Gerda could feel heat make its way up her neck and into her cheeks. She couldn't just stand here and gawk at the man. Why was he still here? Didn't the sheriff tell him what had happened?

"No." Claude's voice penetrated the fog in Gerda's brain. "The freight wagon hasn't come from the station yet. I'm not even sure if the train has arrived. Maybe it's behind schedule."

I have to get out of here. "Thank you, Claude." She wheeled and hurried back to her own store. All the way, she could feel the cowboy's gaze on her back. When she arrived in the workroom, she leaned against the wall and tried to catch her breath. Why didn't the man just leave town? There wasn't anything here for him. She fanned her face with her hand then pressed it to her chest to try to slow her racing heartbeat. If he left right now, it wouldn't be too soon for her.

૨૦

Gerda. Frank rolled her name around in his head as he headed to his hotel room with his purchases from the mercantile. *Gerda Nilsson.* A name that fit her Nordic beauty. If he were to settle here, maybe he could build a relationship with her. Of course, it might not be a good idea. He had experienced so much of the hard side of life, and seen even more, that he wasn't sure he was fit to establish a relationship with a woman like her. She was the kind of woman he had dreamed about all his life, but now that he had met her, he didn't feel worthy.

Frank couldn't stay cooped up in this hotel room, even if it was a nice, large one. He put on his Stetson and stepped out on the boardwalk. He had only seen this end of town and the street down to the livery. If he explored more, maybe he could work off some of his nervous energy.

When he walked by the sheriff's office, the man stepped out the door. After giving Frank an appraising glance, he commented, "You clean up real nice. I would hardly recognize you as the man who came into my office earlier today."

Frank liked the man's wry humor. During their previous discussion, Frank had come to appreciate the older man's thoroughness in dealing with hard topics. "I couldn't go around town looking like I'd been on a cattle drive."

Sheriff Bartlett stepped back a little and gestured toward the interior of the building. "Would you like to come in for a cup of coffee? I keep a pot on the stove. Of course, it won't be as good as you get in the hotel, but it's hot and black."

Frank followed him into the dimly lit room. The sheriff took a clean mug from the shelf on the wall near the stove. After pouring the steaming brew, he handed the white cup to Frank. He took a quick taste. It wasn't bad at all.

"So what are you going to do now?" the sheriff asked after he set his own cup on the desk. "Go back into the marshal service?" Bartlett sat in the chair behind his desk and crossed his booted ankles on top of the desk. He placed his hands behind his head and leaned back, looking Frank straight in the eyes.

Frank dropped into a chair that sat near an open jail cell. "I've considered it."

"You shouldn't have any problem getting back on. Good men are hard to find, and you are persistent," the sheriff added with a chuckle.

Frank glanced out the open door at a wagon that was coming down the street. A man and woman sat on the seat, and several children dangled their legs off the back. "I've been thinking about settling down. I was planning on walking around town. From what I've seen of it, Litchfield might be a good town to settle in."

"Yep," the sheriff agreed. "Most of the time, it is. We don't often have events like the Le Blanc incident." The man dropped his feet back onto the floor with a thud. "How about if I walk along with you? I could give you a personal guided tour."

Frank took a big swig of the cooling beverage and looked down into the nearly empty mug. "You got some place where I can rinse this out?"

"Don't worry about it." Bartlett rose and reached for his hat. "The deputy will take the cups home, and his wife will wash them with her dishes." He led the way out the door.

The sheriff took Frank down the street in the direction he had already been. The lawman introduced him to all of the proprietors along the way.

Soon they arrived at the barbershop. "I really could use a trim." Frank reached up, removed his hat, and pushed some curls off his forehead. Why had he forgotten his hat?

"Let's go in and chat awhile with Silas." Frank followed the sheriff as he stepped through the doorway. "I've brought you a customer," he said to the man behind the chair.

"Just have a seat over there." The barber pointed with his scissors, then he went back to snipping and talking to the man sitting in front of him.

By the time Silas was finished cutting Frank's hair, Frank knew more than he really wanted to know about most of the people in town. What was it about barbers that they liked to talk so much?

"Would you like to go into the saloon?" Sheriff Bartlett asked when they were back out on the sidewalk. "They serve lunch there, and there aren't too many people drinking at this time of day."

Frank followed him through the swinging doors. It had been quite awhile since he had stepped in a saloon. He had forgotten how they smelled. No matter how much they cleaned up a bar, they couldn't get the smell of liquor and tobacco smoke out of the wood. Frank used to like to drink, but he hadn't had time while he was following Le Blanc. He had needed all his wits about him in case he ever found the scoundrel.

A barmaid dressed in red satin brought a bowl of stew and

some corn bread to the two men after they were seated at a round table. She smiled at Frank and leaned over farther than was necessary when she set his food down. Maybe he had been feasting his eyes on pure women long enough that she seemed tawdry and pitiful to him. He turned his attention to his companion, and the woman walked away in a huff. If Frank decided to settle down here, he knew he wouldn't be frequenting this establishment. He started eating quickly, because he wanted the meal over as soon as possible. The sheriff was eating pretty fast, too.

⋆

Once Gerda got her heartbeat to settle down, she decided to close the shop. Anna wasn't coming today, and Gerda had to eat lunch. She went upstairs and pulled out the bread she had made two days before. It didn't look that inviting, but she had to eat something. While she scrambled some eggs, she grilled two pieces of bread in a buttered skillet. Some days she went to the hotel to keep from having to cook for one. August had taken her to the boardinghouse to eat with him several times, too. But today she didn't want to be around other people. Too many things had happened to upset her. For a day that had started with so much promise, it really had deteriorated quickly. The bright part of the day had been spending time with Marissa and Clarissa.

It was wonderful that the sisters were going to have babies. However, that thought brought a sharp pain to Gerda's heart. The pain was followed by the image of the cowboy talking to Claude in the store downstairs. Every detail of how he looked was vivid in her mind's eye. He was no longer dressed like a trail bum. He was even more devastatingly handsome dressed in nice clothes, although curls still fell across his broad forehead, almost reaching his eyes. What was there about him that was different from the other men she had known? They all paled in comparison to his good looks. But looks weren't everything.

After choking down the last of her eggs and toasted bread, Gerda went into the parlor and picked up her Bible. She clutched it to her chest and dropped her chin against it. "Father God, please help me. Please tell me that You have a man picked out for me. I have been patient, but now my desire for a husband and family has brought temptation into my life. I feel undeniably drawn to an unacceptable man. God, please take away the temptation. Father, it would be a blessing if the man would just leave town today. Help me be strong. In Jesus' name, amen."

Gerda knew that God heard her, but the prayer seemed to hang in the air around her. She sighed. When she opened her Bible, it fell open to the sixth chapter of Second Corinthians. Soon, verses 14 through 18 jumped out at her.

Be ye not unequally yoked together with unbelievers: for what fellowship hath righteousness with unrighteousness? and what communion hath light with darkness? and what concord hath Christ with Belial? or what part hath he that believeth with an infidel? and what agreement hath the temple of God with idols? for ye are the temple of the living God; as God hath said, I will dwell in them, and walk in them; and I will be their God, and they shall be my people. Wherefore come out from among them, and be ye separate, saith the Lord, and touch not the unclean thing; and I will receive you, and will be a Father unto you, and ye shall be my sons and daughters, saith the Lord Almighty.

Gerda knew she should not feel drawn to that man. For

some reason, she was sure he was not a Christian. She knew that when God brought a man into her life for her to marry, he wouldn't be an unbeliever. She had to fight this strong attraction she felt for the former lawman.

After sitting there for a few more minutes, Gerda put her Bible on the table beside her rocking chair. She stepped out on the platform at the top of the stairs and turned around to lock her door. As she turned and glanced down the street, she saw the man she had been thinking about come out of the saloon. *It must be a sign from God. He must be showing me that the man is not a godly man.* With a firm nod of her head, she walked down the stairs to open the shop.

❧

When Frank stepped through the swinging doors of the saloon after he and the sheriff had finished their meals, his gaze was drawn to the staircase that led up the side of the mercantile building. Gerda Nilsson stood on the platform at the top, and she was looking his direction. Why had he agreed to go into the saloon with the sheriff? Instinctively he knew she would not like the fact that he was there. It would probably be a setback that would be hard to overcome in his pursuit of the woman of his dreams.

"If you were to settle here, what would you do?" The sheriff's question drew Frank's attention from his thoughts.

"I don't have to go to work immediately. I've saved most of the money I've made over the years. It will give me time to look around and find just the right business to invest in." Frank glanced once again toward the mercantile building, but Gerda was nowhere in sight.

The sheriff walked a few steps without saying anything. "There are a few possibilities. I could introduce you to the owners."

Frank nodded. "That would be nice. And I'm going to need a place to live. Although the hotel is nice, it's not a home."

The sheriff seemed to be lost in thought. After a few minutes of the two men walking back through town, he finally made a suggestion. "I've run down the list of the houses I know to be empty. If you want a wife and family, your best bet might be Mrs. Nichols's home."

"Why do you say that?" Frank's interest was piqued.

"Well, it's pretty new, and it hasn't been lived in very long. Would you like to see it?"

At Frank's agreement, the sheriff led the way to the lawyer's office where they obtained a key to the house, then he accompanied Frank across the railroad tracks and into an area that was mostly homes.

"This area is really pretty." Frank looked at the trees whose branches stretched across the street, almost meeting. "I like all the shade."

Sheriff Bartlett nodded. "That's why I've stayed around here. I think you'll like this house. Oliver Nichols had been a widower for several years. He didn't have any children, so he was lonely. Everyone thought he was crazy when he advertised in several newspapers for a bride."

"Sometimes that works, but sometimes it doesn't," Frank agreed. "Did he get many answers?"

The lawman turned to his right down another tree-lined street. "I don't guess anyone knows how many he got. He didn't share them with anyone. At least we know that a young woman from Ohio answered. They kept up quite a correspondence while Oliver had the house built for her. After it was finished, everyone in town was invited to the large wedding. It was a really happy affair."

"So what happened?"

"They had only lived in the house a few months when Oliver died of a heart attack. His grieving widow soon returned to Ohio to live with her parents."

"How long ago was that?" Frank wondered if the house would be in disrepair, since it had sat empty for a long time.

"It was only a little over a year ago."

The neighborhood was dotted with mature trees that were just beginning to bud. When the sheriff stopped in front of a white wooden fence, Frank turned to look the same direction. Situated at the end of that area of town, the house, which was set back quite a ways from the street, was surrounded by a small grove of trees. Through the nearly bare branches, Frank glimpsed the second story and attic complete with gables and lots of gingerbread decorations. It was just the kind of house that needed a family.

"It doesn't look as though it is vacant." Frank turned toward his companion. "It's been well taken care of."

"The lawyer sees that it is. No one wants to buy a derelict home."

Frank nodded. "I understand that. But why hasn't it sold before now?"

The sheriff led the way up the stepping-stones toward the structure. "It's more house than most new people in town want right away. And the price is a little too high for most folks. I hope that's not a problem for you."

"If I like it, I'm sure the price wouldn't be a deterrent."

After touring the home, Frank knew he was going to buy it. Whether he made any headway with Gerda Nilsson or not, he wanted to live in this house. Someday he'd fill it with a family. The two men started back down the street toward the business part of town so Frank could talk to the lawyer about the house.

"You know," the sheriff said, "maybe the good Lord kept this house available for you. He's been known to do things like that."

Frank didn't know about the "good Lord" part of the sheriff's statement, but he was glad the house was still vacant. After conducting his business with the lawyer, Frank went to the bank to make arrangements to have his money transferred to Litchfield. Then he proceeded to the depot to send a telegram to his bank manager, who was a close family friend, back East. He told him to send the contents of his safe-deposit box in a strongbox on the train. If Frank was going to settle in Litchfield, he needed to have all his assets here.

❧

August came into the Dress Emporium just as Gerda finished giving a customer her new clothes. She went to give her brother a hug when the other woman left the shop.

"I'm glad to see you." She stood back and looked up into his kind eyes. "Is Anna well?"

"Yes. She's fine, just not feeling too good this morning. So she won't be in today."

Gerda moved behind the counter and placed the roll of brown wrapping paper back under it. "You didn't have to come all the way over here just to tell me that. I don't expect her until I see her coming."

August leaned his crossed arms on the polished wood. She knew he did that so they would be closer to the same height. He must have something important to tell her.

She stopped what she was doing and looked at him. "What do you want to talk about?"

"You can read me like a book, can't you?" August gave a nervous laugh.

"So what is it?"

August stood away from the counter and stuffed his hands in the pockets of his trousers, another sure sign of his nervousness. "You know how you told me that you're saving your money to buy Mrs. Nichols's house?"

Gerda nodded. For some reason, she knew she wasn't going to like what he had to say. "I almost have enough for a good down payment. Their lawyer said that I could pay part of it off monthly."

August shuffled his feet. "You can't now."

"And why not?" Gerda wished he'd get to the point instead of talking around a subject.

August looked at the brightly colored fabrics that lined the shelves behind Gerda. He couldn't even look her in the eyes. She sighed. Now she knew she wouldn't want to hear whatever he had to say.

"Frank Daggett bought the house."

"Frank Daggett?" Gerda realized that her question was loud and shrill, but she didn't care. "You mean that cowboy lawman?" Maybe August was wrong. Maybe it wasn't too late for her to buy it. Gerda crossed her arms to keep them from trembling. "How do you know that?"

August patted her on the shoulder. "I know it hurts, but it's true. The sheriff's horse threw a shoe, so he came into the blacksmith shop. He told me about spending the day with Frank showing him around town the other day. Frank wants to settle here, so he bought the house. All the papers are signed, and the money should be here soon."

When August finally left, Gerda wanted to crawl into her bed, pull the quilt up over her head, and cry like a baby. Why did that man have to turn her life upside down again? She had hoped that he would leave town soon, but that wasn't going to happen. What was she going to do now?

As if her thoughts had taken on human form, Frank Daggett walked through the front door of the Dress Emporium. Gerda stood behind the counter and glared at him while he moved around the room, fingering various items on display.

"May I help you, Mr. Daggett?"

The man looked up with eager anticipation, but his face fell when he saw the expression on hers. Gerda didn't care if her sour look drove the man out of the store. What was he here for, anyway? The answer to that question was too much to contemplate. He must have a girlfriend. . .or a wife. Why else would he buy the house?

"Miss Nilsson." The deep baritone voice was much too smooth. "Please call me Frank. I hope we can be friends?"

Gerda ignored the question implied by his voice. "I occasionally make clothing for my brother, who's hard to fit, but you should be able to find things you can wear at the mercantile next door." After this dismissal, Gerda went through the curtains that divided the store from the workroom. She leaned on the wall beside the doorway and waited until she heard the sound of his footsteps as they led to the outside door. When it closed behind the man, she let out the breath she had been holding. What was she going to do now? She had been saving so long to buy that house. She was tired of living in the apartment above the store. If God didn't bring her someone to marry, at least she would have had a real home. But that man had interfered in her life again. Why wouldn't he just go away and leave her alone?

seven

That didn't go very well. Frank berated himself all the way to the hotel. For several days, the words Gerda had blurted in front of the ice cream parlor had never left his mind. They interfered with much of his thinking. Of course she had gotten angry both then and in the sheriff's office, but he thought he had given her enough time to get over it. Surely it was all right to follow up on the feelings she inadvertently had claimed. But the encounter in the Dress Emporium had been far from successful.

Frank knew he didn't understand women very well, but Gerda Nilsson was a complicated puzzle that had him completely baffled. In his thoughts, she was pliant and loving, but when they were face-to-face, she was feisty and often disagreeable. Why was he so drawn to her? He had seen her smile at other people, and that smile could light up a room. Unfortunately, the smile was usually for someone else, not him. She was a combination of grace and beauty. No wonder he couldn't get her out of his mind.

❧

The next morning, Frank ate breakfast at a table near the front window of the restaurant. He realized that when he moved into his house, he would have to cook his own meals. Maybe he would still come here to the hotel. He'd had enough of the few things he knew how to prepare to last a lifetime. Perhaps he could hire a housekeeper who could also cook for him.

When Molly came to pour him more hot coffee, he looked

up from the newspaper he was reading. Out of the corner of his eyes, he noticed a surrey stop in front of the mercantile. Frank was pretty sure the store was closed today. He wondered who it was and why they were there. He guessed he would never lose the habit of watching what was going on, checking for anything out of the ordinary. It was ingrained in him from all the years in law enforcement.

A man and woman were in the surrey. When the man alighted from the carriage, Frank recognized August Nilsson. He climbed the stairs, leaving the woman in the buggy. In just a moment, August and Gerda came down the stairs. All three were dressed up as if they were going somewhere special.

"Is something going on in town today?" Frank looked up at Molly when he asked the question.

The waitress turned and glanced at the trio across the street. "Oh, they're just going to church."

To church? Frank hadn't thought of that. Since he'd become an adult, Frank hadn't had the time or the inclination to attend those meetings.

"Most people in Litchfield go to church on Sundays." Molly looked back at Frank. "I'll be on my way as soon as I finish waiting on you. Cook and I get there a little late and sit on a pew at the back. Can I get you anything else?"

When Frank shook his head, the woman returned to the kitchen, presumably to get ready for church. Frank continued to study the street outside the hotel. There wasn't much activity. What did church have to offer to cause so many people to attend? If he was ever going to understand Gerda, it might be a good thing for him to find out for himself. He really didn't want to make a late entrance, so he wouldn't go today. But next Sunday, he would get up bright and early and see what it was all about.

❧

Gerda could hardly believe her eyes. When she walked into the church, Frank Daggett was already sitting on the pew where her family usually sat. Gerda hoped that August would notice him and choose another place to sit, but he ushered her and Anna into the other end of that pew. Soon Gustaf and Olina and their children joined them. At least they moved into the seat from the other direction. Now they separated her from the man who filled her thoughts so often.

It had been over a week since she had seen him. She was glad about that. Gradually, she had returned to her old self, often forgetting about him for an hour at a time. But she couldn't control her dreams. At night, he cavorted through her mind in a myriad of situations, always her hero. In the morning, she would have to pray especially hard to overcome the temptation he was to her. Now, here he was, sitting a few feet away, and she wondered why. He didn't strike her as a churchgoer. If he were, why hadn't he been here before? He'd been in town more than one Sunday.

The pastor's opening prayer invaded her thoughts. She bowed her head but didn't close her eyes. She peeked at Frank Daggett to see what he was doing. Didn't the man know anything? His head was up, and he watched the pastor with a thoughtful expression on his face. Well, whatever the reason he was here, maybe it would be good for him.

Gerda had a hard time keeping her attention on the service. She was as aware of Frank Daggett as if he were sitting right beside her. When everyone stood, it seemed to take him by surprise, so he was later than anyone else getting to his feet. Although Olina shared a hymnal with the man, he didn't sing a single word. He probably didn't know the songs. Olina had to share her Bible with him when the pastor read from the scriptures, because he didn't have one with him. Gerda was sure the man didn't own one. She wondered if he had ever seen one before. He kept his eyes trained on the words all through the Bible reading. During the sermon, his attention was on the preacher. For someone who may not have been to church before, he didn't seem nervous.

❧

Frank had been a little uncomfortable when the family sat between him and Gerda. He recognized them as the loving couple who had eaten dinner at the hotel with Gerda and August his first night in Litchfield. It didn't take long for the couple to introduce themselves. Gustaf and Olina Nilsson were kin to Gerda and August. They sat with their children between them, and the woman ended up beside him. She was friendly and shared her songbook and Bible with him. Maybe he would need to buy a Bible if he was going to come to church very often. He couldn't rely on the good nature of whoever sat beside him. He wondered if Gerda would have shared hers with him if they were side-by-side. He doubted it. That's why he had stayed out of her way all week. He wanted to know more about this religion thing, since it was so much a part of her life.

"Mr. Daggett." After the final prayer, the petite blond turned toward him.

"Yes, Mrs. Nilsson."

"We would like you to join us for lunch, wouldn't we, Gustaf?" She turned toward her tall husband.

The man looked Frank straight in the eyes. "Of course."

Frank shook his head. "Thank you. I wouldn't want to be any trouble."

"Oh, it's no trouble. We almost always have people come to the house for Sunday lunch. Most of Gustaf's family will be there, as will our friends, the Jensons. I believe you've met some of them, and I gather your first meeting wasn't especially pleasant," she said with a smile. "I want you to have the chance to get to know them better. Besides, I always cook enough for several extra people, just in case."

What could Frank do but agree? He wasn't sure that Gerda would be glad to see him there, but it might be a chance to make progress with her. "Thank you. I'll follow your carriage."

❧

Gerda had seen Olina talking to Frank. Of course, that was just like Olina. She tried to make everyone feel welcome. That was all it was. But when the others started toward Gustaf and Olina's home for Sunday lunch, Gerda was surprised to see Frank Daggett's horse in the procession of buggies. Surely Olina hadn't invited him to have lunch with them. Gerda knew her assumption was probably wrong. Olina often asked visitors to the services to share their noon meal. Why did it have to be Frank Daggett? Gerda sent a prayer for help winging heavenward.

While everyone was exiting their vehicles, Gerda glanced at the house. It no longer looked like the place where Anna and Olina started their dress shop back in 1892. At that time, it had been a small, two-story cottage, but after Olina received an inheritance from her great-aunt Olga, Gustaf had turned the modest house into a large family home, complete with an ample dining room equipped for many guests. All of the existing rooms had been enlarged and other rooms added. Recently, red brick had been applied to the outside walls, and all the windows were framed with white shutters that matched the picket fence surrounding the front yard. Usually, Gerda like to visit her brother and his family. But she dreaded entering the house today.

She wished she hadn't accepted the invitation. She almost hadn't, because all the other adults were couples. However, since they were all so close, she'd never felt like just a single person. Now she wasn't so sure. Perhaps she could plead a headache. All this stress could certainly bring one on quickly. Of course, no one knew how stressed she was about the added guest.

Soon everyone was in the house removing their wraps, and the women went to the kitchen to help Olina. The men entered the parlor. Gustaf took the children with them. Gerda knew that Gustaf and Olina wanted them to be tired enough to nap after the meal. If the men played with them before lunch, then the adults could visit afterward without interruption.

Gerda borrowed one of Olina's large, white ruffled aprons. While she was tying it on, she asked, "Are you sure you feel up to having this many people for lunch?"

Olina removed a large roasting pan from the oven. "Thank you for asking, Gerda, but this time I have more energy than I did before Sven was born. Besides, I really enjoy entertaining."

While the other women put the finishing touches on the meal, Gerda helped Anna set the table. First, they spread out an embroidered linen tablecloth that Olina had brought with her from Sweden. Then they set the good china plates around the sides.

"How many people do we have?" Gerda asked.

Anna started counting them. She stopped before she was finished and took hold of the back of a chair.

Gerda rushed to her side. "Are you all right?"

Anna smiled. "Yes, I was just a little dizzy. It's been awhile since I ate breakfast, and I only had some toast."

"You knew it would be a long time before we had lunch,"

Gerda scolded as she began placing the silverware beside each plate. "Why didn't you eat more?" She glanced up in time to see a blush steal across Anna's cheeks. Gerda put the silverware she was holding on the table in a pile and went to her sister-in-law and best friend. "What aren't you telling me?"

"I'm not telling anyone until I'm sure," Anna whispered. "But I can't keep it from you. Just remember, this is our secret. I haven't even told August what I suspect."

Gerda pulled Anna into a hug. "I'm so happy for you. I know how much you've wanted a baby. I will pray that it's true."

Anna reached up and wiped a tear from the corner of her eye. "I know. It's too wonderful."

Gerda went back to placing the silverware beside the other plates. She knew that she should be glad for August and Anna, and she was. But her happiness for them mingled with sadness for herself. What was wrong with her? When she looked in the mirror, the woman who gazed back at her wasn't unattractive. She had always been a pleasant companion, hadn't she? Why was she still unmarried? A tear slipped from her eye, and it wasn't a tear of happiness as Anna's had been.

❧

Frank stayed in the background in the parlor while August and Gustaf played with the two blond children. Gustaf had a wonderful family with another child on the way. What did Frank have to show for all his years as a lawman? Now that he owned a house, maybe the wife and family wouldn't be far behind. He enjoyed watching the interaction between the children and their father. Olga, the little girl, loved her uncle August, too. He picked her up and swung her high into the air. Her peals of laughter were a balm to Frank's weary soul. He had just begun to feel comfortable in this home when the women called them to the table.

When Frank saw the bounty spread before them, he was amazed. He hadn't had a feast like this in years, even on holidays, and this was just Sunday lunch. The mingling aromas teased his senses, making him suddenly ravenous. Having a home and family could provide these kinds of blessings to him, too. That thought caused his gaze to seek out Gerda. He didn't like what he saw. For some reason, tears glistened in her eyes. He wished he had the right to go across the room, take her in his arms, and comfort her.

Olina told each person where to sit, and they took their places. Frank was amazed that the room didn't feel crowded, even with all the people clustered around the table. He had been introduced to Ollie and Lowell Jenson in the living room. The brothers looked almost as much alike as their twin wives, Clarissa and Marissa, did. All these other people were related in various ways, yet Frank didn't feel like an outsider. This family was so warm and friendly.

Gustaf pronounced a blessing on the meal. Frank remembered blessings spoken at mealtime while his mother was still alive but not one had sounded as if the person speaking them was talking to a friend the way Gustaf's did. As the hostess started passing dishes around the table, group conversation started.

"I wish I had been there to see their faces when you drew your guns on these three women." With a twinkle in his eyes, Ollie Jenson looked right at Frank.

Frank was surprised. He thought these men would be upset with him, but they didn't seem to be. "If I had known the truth at that time, I never would have done it. I apologize."

He glanced at Gerda, who was seated across the table from him. She watched him with amazement in her expression. A large mirror with a heavy gold frame hung on the wall behind her. Frank saw not only her beautiful face, but also the reflection of the back of her dainty head. Everything about her caused a tightening in his gut. What was he going to have to do to get her to forgive him and return to the feelings that had connected them across the hotel lobby?

"What did you think when August threw his arm around your neck?" the other Jenson brother asked with a smile.

"At first, I thought there must be more to the Le Blanc gang than I had suspected. I knew Pierre didn't have that much strength. It was all I could do to keep from passing out."

August looked sheepish. "I wasn't trying to hurt you. I was only protecting our women."

"And I don't blame you. I would have done the same thing in your place."

The other men agreed.

"At that point I decided it might be time to hang up my guns. I had already turned in my badge, and I had never let a woman get the drop on me before."

Laughter echoed around the room, but Gerda didn't join in. Frank could tell that she was trying to digest all he said. Would he ever be able to reach her and see her return to being the warm, animated woman he had observed that first day? Something was really bothering her. Was it his presence? Maybe he should finish eating and go back to the hotel to allow her to enjoy the rest of the day with her family and friends.

"So, Frank." Olina looked down the table toward where he sat halfway between herself and her husband at the other end. "What are you going to do if you hang up your guns?"

Every eye in the room was trained on him. Frank cleared his throat. "I've been talking to the sheriff about investing in a business, but we haven't come up with the right one yet."

"But he did help you buy Mrs. Nichols' house." August's statement was not a question. He must know all about it.

Frank nodded. "He was kind enough to take me on a tour of the house after he introduced me to Harold Jones. Then Mr. Jones and I worked out the details. Are you familiar with the house?"

"Yes," August answered. "Actually, Gerda was trying to save enough money to make a down payment on it."

"You were?" Olina asked her sister-in-law. "We didn't know that. We would have helped you."

Frank looked at Gerda. The tears were back, glistening in her eyes.

"I wanted to do it on my own."

The words hung in the air between them, and suddenly Frank understood just how important that house was to Gerda. Without knowing it, he had done something else to hurt her. He wished there were some way he could make it up to her. If he thought she would accept it, he would sign over the deed to her today. But he knew she wouldn't. Maybe he could sell it to her himself, but he didn't want to profit from her, and he somehow knew she wouldn't buy it any other way.

"I understand that house is unfurnished, Mr. Daggett." Anna Nilsson reached out and took Gerda's hand as if giving her a lifeline. "What are you going to do for furniture?"

Frank looked around the table. Everyone seemed to be genuinely interested in his answer. "When my parents died, I inherited all their household goods. It's stored in a warehouse my uncle owns in Philadelphia. I've already sent a letter to my uncle telling him to ship everything to me. I realize it might not be enough to fill that house, but it will be a good start. It should arrive soon."

❧

Gerda felt as if a boulder had lodged itself near her heart. Not only had he bought her house, the man had furniture to fill it. All of her dreams evaporated like a mist in the morning sunlight. She wanted to excuse herself and leave the room, but she knew that Olina would be hurt if she didn't eat more of the wonderful food than she already had. However, she didn't know how she could get it past the gigantic lump in her chest.

"Mr. Daggett." Olina gestured at each woman around the table. "We are so glad that you've decided to settle in our town. We'd like to help you clean up the house before your furniture arrives, wouldn't we?"

The other women started talking at once, agreeing with her. All except Gerda. Somehow she couldn't push words past the heaviness, either. She knew it would look bad if she didn't help them, but she couldn't agree. Not today, anyway.

"I appreciate your offer, but why don't we wait until my furniture arrives. Then the house would be fresh to move it into."

The man's words made sense, but they didn't change the way Gerda felt. Her world was slowly crumbling around her, and she didn't know what to do about it.

eight

Frank was pleased that the women had offered to help him prepare his house for the arrival of his possessions. It gave him a feeling of acceptance and finally belonging somewhere. He'd expected Gerda to object, but she didn't. She didn't exactly say that she would help, but she didn't say she wouldn't either. Because she hadn't refused, a tiny flame of hope ignited in Frank's heart—hope that there could be a future for him and Gerda. If he were a praying man, he might ask God to help him, but he wasn't even on speaking terms with God, if there was one. By starting to go to church, he was doing his best to find out if God was real.

It only took a week for the strongbox to arrive with what Frank had stored in his safe-deposit box back East. The banker had also put the money Frank had in his savings account in the box. The key to the strongbox had arrived on the previous train, enclosed in a package addressed to Frank. After he got home and opened the box, he carried it to the bank, wrapped in brown paper. He didn't want to announce the fact that he had a strongbox with him.

"I'd like to talk to the bank manager, please," Frank told the teller when he arrived.

The man went into a back room, then returned accompanied by a spry man wearing a black suit and glasses. "I'm Mr. Finley. What can I do for you, sir?" the manager asked.

"I'm Frank Daggett. Could I speak to you privately, Mr. Finley?"

The manager led Frank into an office lined with dark paneled walls. The furniture in the room could have graced the bank office back East. It gave Frank confidence that this was a prosperous bank.

"I would like to open an account." Frank sat in the wine-colored leather chair across from Mr. Finley. "I would also like to put this strongbox in your safe. It contains some of my family valuables."

The banker smiled at him. "We'd be glad to accommodate you. How much money would you like to deposit in your account?"

When Frank told him, the man's smile broadened. He rose from his chair and extended his hand. "We'll be glad to have you as a customer, Mr. Daggett."

When they had finished the paperwork, Mr. Finley took Frank into the vault. He proudly displayed its strength, reassuring Frank that it was completely safe.

❧

After that first Sunday when Frank went to church, he had friends in town besides the sheriff. He often saw one or more of the men, and they always included him in conversations and expressed a genuine interest in what was happening with him. Frank couldn't remember a time since he'd become an adult when he'd had true friends. It felt good.

Frank continued to attend church, but he wasn't sure he understood what the preacher was talking about. He had never been one to make any kind of decision without a lot of thought. He listened intently, trying to get a handle on what this religion business was all about.

One Monday, Frank decided to exercise his horse by taking a ride away from town. He took a different direction from any he had taken before. After he had ridden awhile, he came to a place with a wrought iron arch over the entrance. Worked into the arch were the words JENSON HORSE FARM. *This must be owned by Lowell and Ollie.* He turned under the archway and rode up the drive toward a large, white farmhouse surrounded by magnificent stables. He had heard that theirs was the most successful horse farm in five states. Now he understood why. The animals that ran across the surrounding pastures were sleek. Their shiny coats glistened in the morning sunlight. Several colts cavorted after their mothers. For a moment, he stopped his horse and watched. Their manes and tails waved in the wind as they raced across the greening fields.

When he rode up to the house, a pleasant-looking older woman stepped out onto the porch. "May I help you?" she asked as she brushed a wisp of hair up away from the back of her neck with one hand.

Frank tipped his hat. "Good morning, ma'am. I'm Frank Daggett. I was just out riding and noticed the sign. I thought I would stop and visit with Lowell and Ollie."

The woman moved to the top step and used her other hand to shade her eyes from the bright morning sun. A gentle breeze blew her skirt around her ankles. "Oh, Mr. Daggett. I've heard about you. I'm Margreta Jenson, the boys' mother."

Frank dismounted and stood at the bottom of the steps. He removed his hat and ran his fingers through his hair to push the curls back from his forehead. "I'm sure you have. I'm very sorry about the misunderstanding with your daughters-in-law."

Mrs. Jenson smiled. "We've all gotten a good laugh out of that. But we understand why you did what you did. We're just glad that it had already been taken care of."

The sound of hoofbeats coming down the drive captured their attention. They both turned to look. A man with a star pinned to his chest was making his way toward them.

"Oh, Sheriff Bartlett." The woman standing on the porch suddenly sounded a little breathless.

Frank looked at her. One of her hands fluttered to her throat, and she looked somehow younger and more animated than she had while he was talking to her. He glanced toward the sheriff and caught him smiling at her. *Well, well, perhaps I'm not the only one trying to pursue a woman.*

"Good morning, Sheriff." Frank greeted his friend. "What brings you out here today?"

For a moment the man didn't answer. He seemed to be having a hard time taking his gaze off the woman on the porch. Then he turned to Frank.

"I've come to have lunch. Mrs. Jenson invited me."

"We'd be glad to have you join us, Mr. Daggett." Her voice sounded softer and gentler than before.

Frank glanced from one of them to the other. "Thank you, but I think I'll pass. Are Lowell and Ollie around?"

"They're working with the horses in the barn." She gave a vague wave toward the buildings behind the house.

Frank returned his hat to his head. "Thank you, Mrs. Jenson, for the information." He tied his horse to the hitching post in front of the house and started toward the barn. He could hear soft conversation going on behind him, and he smiled. He wondered if Lowell and Ollie realized the sheriff was interested in their mother and she welcomed it.

Frank placed one foot on the bottom rail of the fence then leaned his forearms on the top. Ollie was putting a horse through its paces.

Lowell joined Frank. "What brings you out here today?"

"I was just out for a ride when I noticed the name over your gate." Frank smiled at him. "I thought I'd drop in and see the horse farm I had heard so much about. You have a nice spread here."

"We think so."

Ollie led the animal close to where the other two men leaned on the fence. "Say, Frank, have you decided what you're going to do yet?"

Frank stood back from the fence and shoved his hands in the front pockets of his denim trousers. "Not yet. I'm still looking around."

Ollie tied the lead rope loosely to the top rail. "We have a neighbor who wants to sell his farm."

"Yeah, he wants to move to California," Lowell added. "We thought you might be interested in buying it."

Frank studied the grass that grew around the fence post nearby. "I'm not sure that's quite what I'm looking for. I don't want to be this far from town."

Although his grandfather was a farmer, Frank hadn't spent much time learning about farming from him, and he died when Frank was pretty young.

After Ollie turned the young horse he was working with out into the pasture, he stood in the doorway to the barn. "Lowell and I are going over to my house for lunch. Marissa is there with Clarissa, and they're fixing something special. They wouldn't tell us what. You're welcome to join us."

Frank glanced up toward the house where the sheriff and Mrs. Jenson had entered. "You don't all live here?"

Ollie watched his boot as he scuffed the dirt by the door. "We had a real misunderstanding before we found out the truth about Marissa and Clarissa. During that time, I started building my own home on the other side of our property. Now Clarissa and I live there."

Lowell glanced up at the main house. "Besides, we wanted

to give Mother and the sheriff a little privacy."

Frank looked from one brother to the other. "I wondered if you knew that they were interested in each other. I also wondered how you felt about it."

"Our father passed away awhile ago." Lowell stopped to clear his throat. "The sheriff was helpful with the girls while all the trouble with their stepfather was going on, and he spent time out here at the farm. I guess you could say that this relationship is another blessing that came from all that happened."

Ollie smiled. "Lowell and I are so happy in our marriages that we want *Mor* to be happy, too."

❧

Just before he reached town, Frank's horse threw a shoe. It was a good thing they were close to town, because Frank wouldn't have wanted to walk too far. Although it was May, the days had started heating up a lot by midday. He didn't want to ride the horse while the hoof wasn't protected. He just hoped August wouldn't be too busy to make a new shoe today.

When Frank walked through the door of the smithy, August turned to greet him. "It's good to see you again." The burly man wiped his right hand on his apron then stuck it toward Frank.

He shook the proffered hand. "I'm afraid this isn't a social call. My horse threw a shoe just outside town. Do you think you could get to it today?"

August turned and went out through the open doorway. "He's a magnificent animal." The big man crooned something into the horse's ear and scratched his head. "Have you had him long?"

Frank patted his animal's neck. "We've been together quite awhile. He's been more than just transportation for me. Sometimes he was my only companion."

August ran his hand down each leg until he came to the one the horse was favoring. He lifted the hoof and looked at it. "I can fix this right now, if you want to wait."

After following the blacksmith into the warm building, Frank leaned against a table by the wall. It was close enough to the door that he could feel a slight breeze. August was using some kind of aromatic wood in the forge today. It took away from the unpleasant smoky odor that Frank usually associated with smithies. He watched the other man look through a pile of horseshoes until he found the one he wanted. When he went back out and picked up the unshod hoof and measured it against the horseshoe he had chosen, it was almost a perfect fit. After taking the piece of formed iron to the forge, he held it in the flames with long tongs.

"So have you found a business to invest in?" August looked at Frank, instead of the metal that was slowly heating.

"Not yet."

"I don't know if you'd be interested, but Hank over at the livery mentioned that he was thinking about selling. He hasn't been the same since he was burned out last summer. Even though he built the stable back, his heart isn't in it anymore. Would you like to talk to him about purchasing it?"

Frank let his chin rest against his chest while he thought about it. After a moment, he raised his gaze toward the fire, where the horseshoe was beginning to glow. "I don't think I'd be any good at running a livery stable either."

August pulled the horseshoe from the fire and took it to the anvil. He only had to pound it a few times to get it to the shape he wanted, but the loud noise prevented further conversation for a time. After the metal was the shape he wanted, he plunged it into a bucket of cold water. A loud hiss accompanied the steam that rose from the bucket.

"I'll keep an ear open when people are talking." August turned to smile at him. "I sure wouldn't want you to leave here now. We're getting used to having you around." With a chuckle, he lifted the horseshoe out of the water and tested the temperature of the metal. Then he went outside to where the horse was tied.

"Thanks. I like it here, too." Frank accompanied him outside. It was fascinating to watch the man. He was like an artist, knowing just where to put the nails to protect the horse and pounding them in with a minimum of strokes.

When he was finished, Frank paid August, then rode his horse over to the livery. When he got back to the other side of the railroad tracks, Frank decided to make another visit to the Dress Emporium. It had been too long since he had seen Gerda. Even though she didn't seem to be interested in him, he wasn't going to give up. He still remembered the words that had burst from her lips the day she'd held the gun on him. They warmed his heart whenever he felt lonely.

⁂

Gerda couldn't believe that Frank Daggett was back in the Dress Emporium again. It seemed as though he was always underfoot. This time, he talked to Anna. Gerda tried to look disinterested, but his gaze kept straying toward her, even though he was talking to her friend. Picking up a bolt of fabric, Gerda made her way through the curtains into the workroom. There was no hurry to cut out the new outfit that Marja Braxton ordered today, but taking the fabric into the back room gave Gerda a good excuse to leave the area where Frank was. Unfortunately, even from the back room, Frank's melodious voice penetrated Gerda's heart.

She sat on the padded chair in front of the sewing machine and leaned her elbows on the table. Gerda buried her face in her hands and prayed as hard as she could for the Lord to deliver her from the temptation that was Frank Daggett. When she finished and raised her head, she could still hear him discussing yesterday's church service with Anna. The man had been attending services for several weeks. How could he listen to the powerful sermons without becoming a believer? Was he just making a show of being interested in church for some nefarious reason? Of course, he wasn't anything like Pierre Le Blanc had been. When Pierre was in church, he didn't even try to look interested. Frank listened intently to the sermons. He had even started trying to sing some of the songs, but as far as Gerda could tell, he still didn't have his own Bible. He usually sat with Gustaf and Olina, and whoever was nearest to Frank shared a Bible with him.

She got up and put the bolt of fabric on the cutting table. While she measured the amount needed to complete Marja's new suit, her thoughts were filled with Frank. Since that day when he'd tried to arrest her and the twins, Gerda had never seen him dressed like a cowboy. He always wore nice clothes when he came by. His trousers and shirts looked as though they were tailored just for him. She wondered if he already owned them or if he had bought them at the mercantile. She would ask Marja, but Gerda knew that it would only cause Marja to ask questions she didn't want to answer to herself, much less to anyone else.

It was a wonder Gerda was able to cut the fabric straight. Those icy blue eyes, surrounded by long black lashes, twinkled as they looked at her in her mind's eye. Her hands still itched to reach out and brush back the curls that often fell over his forehead. He'd had more than one haircut since he came to town, but nothing tamed those curls. Some men didn't keep their hair especially clean, or else they put too much hair cream on it, so it looked greasy. Frank's never did. Gerda wondered what it would feel like to run her fingers through those curly strands, especially where the hair in the back reached his collar and curled up slightly. She imagined that if she put her arms around his shoulders, she would be able to feel their texture.

Disgusted with herself, Gerda slammed the scissors down on the cutting table. Then she realized that the voices in the next room had silenced. She turned and stared into the face of her best friend, who stood framed between the curtains that divided the room, a shocked expression on her face.

"Gerda!" Anna came all the way into the workroom. "Are you going to tell me what's the matter?"

Gerda didn't want to upset Anna, considering her condition, but what could she tell her?

"I've noticed that you aren't very nice to Mr. Daggett when he comes to the store."

"Just why would he be coming into a women's clothing store, anyway?" Gerda knew her voice was harsh, but she couldn't keep it from sounding that way. "It's not as if he ever buys anything."

Anna patted Gerda on the arm. "I think he just needs friends. Why don't you want to be his friend?"

Unfortunately, "friends" was not what Gerda wanted to be with Frank Daggett. Much to her shame, she wanted more. She had carried this burden in her heart too long. Anna was one of her best friends as well as her sister-in-law, and Anna had taken Gerda into her confidence about the baby, long before she told anyone else. If Gerda could tell anyone about what was bothering her, it was Anna.

She turned and looked at Anna. "Can I tell you something in confidence?"

"Of course you can." Anna sat in the chair by the windows. "I'm ready to listen. You have my full attention."

Gerda dropped into the chair by the sewing machine. "I'm not sure how to say this."

Anna leaned forward. "Just start at the beginning."

"I haven't told anyone, but the first time I saw Frank Daggett was the day August and I had dinner with Gustaf and Olina."

"I didn't know that." Anna leaned back and smiled.

"He was coming down the stairs in the hotel lobby while we were waiting for Gustaf and Olina to arrive. I glanced up," Gerda said as a blush moved up her cheeks, "and when our eyes met, it was as if everything within me connected with everything in him. I don't know how to explain it. For a moment, I felt as if we were the only two people in the room."

Anna looked as if she were holding back a chuckle. "That's interesting."

Gerda got up and walked to the window nearest the sewing machine. She held back the curtain and gazed at nothing in particular. "Don't you see? All these years I've waited for God to bring me someone to love, and the only person I've felt anything special for is a man who isn't a Christian. I've been praying for God to take the temptation from me. I just can't get too close to him, because. . ."

After a moment, Anna asked, "Because what?"

Gerda turned away and crossed her arms. "I'm afraid I could fall in love with him very easily. I can't risk that."

❧

When Anna arrived the next morning, she was carrying her Bible. Gerda watched her sit in the chair by the windows and open the book.

"I prayed about you last night. When I started reading the

Bible, I found this verse, and it spoke to me about Frank Daggett. Do you want to hear it?"

When Gerda nodded, Anna opened the book to where she had a bookmark. " 'And the Lord said unto Satan, Hast thou considered my servant Job, that there is none like him in the earth, a perfect and an upright man, one that feareth God, and escheweth evil?' That verse describes Frank."

"Read it to me again." Gerda wanted to be sure she heard it right.

Anna read it another time. "That's how Mr. Daggett is. He is an upright man, and he has fought evil all of his life."

"I don't know about that part about him fearing God. I haven't seen any indication of that."

Anna closed her Bible and laid it on the small table that sat near the chair she was using. "He listens to every word the preacher says. If he doesn't know God yet, I'm sure he will soon. You know, Gerda, maybe Frank *is* the man God brought to you."

This statement startled Gerda. She paced across the room. That was something she hadn't even considered. Why would God bring that man to her when there were so many other godly men around? But none of them had ever caused her pulse to race the way it did around Frank Daggett.

Gerda turned back toward her friend. "I saw him coming out of the saloon one day."

"When was that?"

"Soon after he came to town."

"But have you seen him go into the saloon since he started coming to church?"

Gerda thought about it a moment. She had only seen him at the saloon that one time. Could she be wrong about him?

nine

Frank was sure he would never make any headway with Gerda. Every time he went to the Dress Emporium, she wasn't very friendly. Anna Nilsson always made him feel welcome, but Gerda was either almost rude to him, or she hid in the back room. Not only had he scared and insulted her when he tried to arrest her, he'd unknowingly bought her dream house. What did a man have to do to make up for the mistakes he inadvertently made? He never meant to hurt her.

Frank was walking toward the bank when the sheriff joined him. "I'd really like to talk to you. Would you join me in my office for a cup of coffee? Or should we go to the restaurant in the hotel?"

"Your coffee is fine with me." Frank followed his friend into the building.

After pouring each of them a mugful of the brew, Sheriff Bartlett dropped into his chair behind the desk. He gathered the papers scattered across the top, formed them into a neat stack, and placed them to the side. Then he leaned his forearms on the smooth surface of the desk.

"I'm thinking about retiring."

Frank knew that wasn't the whole story, so he waited to let the man tell it in his own good time. Frank dropped into the other chair and propped one booted foot on his other knee.

"I'm thinking about buying a small farm that's for sale outside town. It wouldn't be too much for me to take care of, and it has a nice little house on it."

Frank crossed his arms over his chest and looked at the older man. "Sounds good, if that's what you want to do."

"There's more to it than that." The sheriff leaned back and gazed off into the distance. "I'm thinking about getting married."

"Mrs. Jenson?"

The lawman nodded. "I knew you probably had that one figured out. I don't want to ask Margreta to marry me while I'm still a lawman. I'm getting too old for this, and I want to enjoy a life with less danger."

"Just how much danger is there here in Litchfield?" Frank hadn't seen much since he'd arrived. Even the men who frequented the saloon didn't cause much of a disturbance.

"Not a lot." Sheriff Bartlett wiped his hand across his clean-shaven jaw. "The worse that has happened since I've been here was the Le Blanc incident. It could have turned ugly and anything could have gone wrong, but it didn't."

Frank mulled over what the man had said. "Why are you telling me all this?"

"Well, I've watched you as you've considered businesses to invest in. Nothing has appealed to you. I think it's because you're still a lawman at heart. Besides, you're a lot younger than I am."

Frank placed his foot back on the floor and laughed. "Some days I feel younger, but some days I feel older."

"I know what you mean. You sure do see the hard side of life when you're a lawman, but I don't think that's a problem here. Litchfield is a nice, quiet town, and since you want to settle here, it might be a good opportunity for both of us to get what we want. I can't retire until there's someone to take my place, and I won't ask her to share that life with me. She's already lost one husband."

"What about your deputy?"

"Clarence isn't interested in being sheriff. He says being deputy is enough for him."

Frank got up and rubbed one finger across his mustache. "Can you give me a little time to think about it?"

"Sure." The sheriff smiled. "Just don't take too long. I'm not getting any younger."

❧

Business in the Dress Emporium grew almost every week. Gerda liked to keep busy. That way she didn't have too much time to think about Frank Daggett. But she still couldn't get the man out of her mind. No wonder. Every time she turned around, there he was—at church, in the shop, or with her close friends. It wasn't enough that he had taken away the house she had dreamed of buying, now he seemed to be taking all her friends, too.

Anna was a little late coming in on Wednesday. She had started trying to work every day to help Gerda with the added business. "I'm sorry I'm late." Anna breezed through the door. "I had another bout of sickness this morning. I finally was able to keep some toast down."

Gerda looked up from straightening the things that were in disarray under the counter. "If you don't feel like working, I'll understand."

Anna stopped at the end of the counter and peered down at what Gerda was doing. "I'm fine now, and we have so much to do. I want to finish the suit for Mother. I wish she would just let me make things for her at home instead of coming in and insisting on paying for them like any other customer."

Gerda lifted the cash box and placed it on the counter. Using the key attached to the inside of her belt, she opened it. "I need to go to the bank. I didn't have time last week.

Now the box is almost overflowing. I don't like keeping this much cash in the store."

"Why don't you go while I work on the suit?"

Gerda had a special, larger reticule in which she carried money to the bank. She didn't want it to look like a money-bag and tempt someone to try to steal it from her on the way. She went into the back room and took the special handbag off the shelf. Then she stuffed the bills into the bottom of the bag and added a handkerchief on top of the money.

"I'll be back soon," she called to Anna, who was now in the workroom.

It was a pretty day. May was still spring, but it felt more like summer. The trees were covered with leaves, and flowers were blooming in several flower beds around town. Gerda loved spring. All the fresh, new growth reminded her that life could be renewed, too. So what if she couldn't buy her dream house. God probably had something else just as wonderful in mind for her. Because she had a lot of money saved, she decided to start looking at other houses that were for sale. Maybe one of them would be just right for her. Anyway, the one Frank bought would have been too large for a single woman living alone.

When she went into the bank, there was a short line at the teller's window. Gerda didn't want anyone to figure out that she was carrying the cash from the store, so she patiently waited until no one else was in line. She glanced around the room and noticed a stranger standing near the door. His hat was pulled low over his brow, so she couldn't tell too much about him. She wondered if he was someone new moving to town. Litchfield did seem to be growing a lot lately.

Soon it was her turn to make a deposit. The teller had just greeted her when she felt something hard touch the middle of her back. Even through the material of her dress, it was cold.

"Don't move," a grating, masculine voice sounded close to her ear.

She started to turn and look at the man, but the hard thing pushed deeper into her back, and she knew it had to be a gun barrel. She couldn't believe a man was holding a gun on her again. For some reason, she felt more apprehensive now than she had the last time. She had known that Frank wouldn't pull the trigger, but she wasn't sure about this stranger. If she could have just seen the expression in his eyes, maybe she would have been able to tell. Cold fingers of fright danced up and down her spine. It took all her willpower to keep from shivering. It was a good thing that her reticule was hanging safely on her arm, or she might have dropped it.

"Don't move." The man turned his attention toward the teller, who stood as if paralyzed behind the metal bars of the teller's cage. "And you there, come around and lock the front door. You do have a key to the front door, don't you?"

The poor teller was shaking so badly he could hardly get the key into the lock. Gerda could hear it scrape around on the metal, and the vibrations from the man were almost tangible in the room. Mr. Jackson was an elderly man who had been at the bank as long as Gerda had lived in the area. As far as she knew, he had worked there long before, as well. When he turned around after securing the door, he returned to his post with his trembling hands raised. His face had blanched almost white. Gerda was afraid the poor man was going to pass out right there.

"Where is the bank manager?" The gruff voice was louder this time.

Mr. Jackson's voice wavered, then became a whisper. "He's in his office."

"Go get him, but if either of you does anything foolish,

this woman will not see another day."

Gerda didn't like the sound of that. She could tell from the steely tone of his voice that the man meant every word he said. She had never fainted in her life, but she felt the color drain from her own face. Without moving her body, she took hold of the counter in front of her with her hands to keep from slipping away. She took a deep breath and slowly let it out, trying to gain control of her emotions and her reluctant body.

"How can I hel—" Mr. Finley's question died when he saw the man holding his gun on Gerda.

"If you do what I say, this woman won't be hurt."

Following the robber's instructions, Mr. Finley went into the safe and brought out bags of money. Then he unlocked the door to the alley. Two other bandits entered wearing bandannas pulled over their mouths and noses. They started picking up the bags of money and carrying them outside, presumably to load on their horses. A wagon would be too slow for a quick getaway.

When they had loaded all the bags, the leader told one of them to go into the vault with Mr. Finley and make sure they had all the money. After they returned and told him they had it, the two other bandits went out the back door.

"Let's see what you have in that bag." The robber ripped Gerda's reticule from where she carried it on her arm. "You were here to make a deposit, weren't you?" Gerda looked from her handbag to the robber's face, which was now covered with a handkerchief as the other men's had been. "Well, this is quite a haul right here." He stuffed the bag inside his shirt and gestured with his gun. "The three of you come inside here and lie facedown on the floor."

They went into the teller's cage area and complied.

"What time does your watch say, Banker?"

Mr. Finley fumbled to pull the watch out of its pocket. After telling the robber what he wanted to know, he stuffed it back into its place. The fob fell against the floor making a loud thud in the stillness.

"Take that watch back out. I want you to keep an eye on it, Banker. Don't anyone move for at least fifteen minutes. I'm going to leave one man watching you from outside the back door. If anyone moves, the woman will be shot first."

When she heard the horses ride away, Gerda almost started crying, but she was afraid it would cause the gunman to shoot. The only thing she knew to do was pray.

&

All Frank could think about since the sheriff had talked to him was whether he should become sheriff or not. In one way, it was tempting. He had always been a good lawman. But would it prevent him from having a normal life with the woman he was coming to love? Even if she wouldn't give him the time of day.

Every time he laid his eyes on her, her beauty assailed him. But there was more to Gerda than outward appearances. Her beauty was internal as well. He'd heard all the sayings. Beauty is only skin deep. Beauty is as beauty does. She exemplified all of them—with everyone except him. He only hoped that she would soon forgive him for the pain he had caused her. Frank had waited a long time to settle down. He could wait even longer for a woman like Gerda Nilsson.

Frank had looked into several business ventures, but none appealed to him. Of course, he had enough money saved to live a long time without having to work, but he wanted to be busy doing something worthwhile. And what was more worthwhile than serving as sheriff for this quiet town? In Litchfield, he should be able to both serve as a lawman and be a family man. Other men did it.

When Frank and the sheriff had finished their discussion, Frank went back to his room at the hotel to think. He didn't want to be distracted by all the activities in town. Finally, he knew that he couldn't make the decision today, so he started back toward the bank to make a withdrawal since he had spent almost all the money he had been carrying. Just before he reached the bank, the front door burst open and three people rushed out. Mr. Finley, the bank manager; Mr. Jackson; and Gerda—and something was definitely wrong.

"There's been a bank robbery!" Gerda ran to him and grabbed the front of his shirt, holding on as if it were a lifeline. "They took all my money!" Then she burst into tears.

Of their own volition, Frank's arms went around her and cradled her head against his chest. He was glad when she didn't pull away. Instead, she nestled close enough that her tears soaked through his shirt, but he didn't care. She was finally in his arms. Then he realized what she was saying.

"He pulled a gun on me, and he threatened to shoot me, and he took all the money in the bank, and he took my bag with the Dress Emporium money in it, and he made us lie down on the floor!" Gerda's rambling was punctuated with sobs.

Frank heard the banker and the bank teller both shout, "I'm going to get the sheriff!" Then the two men ran down the boardwalk, their boots making thudding sounds that resonated up and down the street. Other people turned to stare, both at the men running and at Frank as he held Gerda. He didn't want to destroy her reputation, so he released his arms from around her and started patting her back.

"It's going to be all right. They've gone for the sheriff."

By the time Frank got the words out, the sheriff, accompanied by Mr. Finley and Mr. Jackson, ran toward the bank.

The three men went in the open front door of the bank. Frank turned Gerda around, and the two of them joined the men inside.

The sheriff questioned all three of the people who were there during the robbery. "We'll need to send a posse after them right away." He turned to Frank. "Have you ever headed up a posse?"

Frank nodded.

"This robbery could be a diversion," Sheriff Bartlett whispered as he scratched his head. "That's all I can say except that I don't think Deputy Wright and I should leave town, just in case someone's planning another robbery, if you get my drift. Would you be willing to lead the posse?"

"I'll help any way I can." Frank wondered if perhaps the sheriff was expecting a courier or a shipment containing something valuable today.

A large crowd had formed in the street in front of them. August Nilsson and Hank from the livery stood near the front of the group. Frank motioned for the two men to come up on the boardwalk where he and the sheriff stood.

"We need a posse, but I don't want too many people." He placed his hand on August's massive shoulder. "You know these people better than I do. I want you and Hank and four other men who are strong, intelligent, and have cool heads."

August surveyed the crowd. He pointed out each person. "Harold Jones is real levelheaded. Silas is a good rider and shoots straighter than most anyone in the county. Harvey and Charles Stevenson own the farm next to ours. They will do whatever you need them to."

Frank motioned to each man August recommended, and they quickly stepped up beside him. "I'd like you to be part of the posse."

They all nodded in agreement.

Frank hadn't noticed that the sheriff had gone until he returned carrying a deputy's badge.

"Frank, you can't go without me deputizing you." He pinned the star to Frank's chest.

Frank looked down at it. A small lump formed in his throat. It felt so good to be wearing a badge again, even if it was just temporary.

≈

For whatever reason, the robbers weren't careful to cover their tracks very well. It didn't take the posse long to pick up the trail.

August rode beside Frank, their horses never breaking stride as the men shouted to one another. "I think I know where they're headed."

"Where?"

"They're going in the direction that leads to the place where Pierre Le Blanc kept his hidden camp."

Frank halted the posse, so they could strategize. "How hard is it to find this place?"

August stopped his mount beside Frank's. "You have to know what you're looking for. That's why it's a perfect hideout."

"Does anyone here know how to get there?"

August's horse took one side step. The high-strung animals sensed the excitement and urgency of their riders. "I've been there. Lowell and Ollie showed it to me after Le Blanc was captured."

After August described to Frank the surrounding territory, Frank divided the other men into three groups of two. They rode to the valley as quietly as possible. Then they left their horses tied at the outer edge of the woods. Soon the seven men worked their way toward the clearing in the center of the valley. They spread out along the perimeter of forest, being careful to stay hidden in the undergrowth.

Sure enough, the three robbers lounged around a campfire. Two counted the money, and one stood guard. Frank signaled the other posse members to move around the perimeter of the woods until they were all near the campsite, which was off to one side of the clearing.

Frank didn't want to jump the gun. He wanted to make an arrest without anyone coming to harm. He hunkered down to watch through the bushes. When the two robbers finished sorting the cash, they started dividing it.

"I want a larger cut." The tall, lean man spoke with a gravelly voice. "This job was my idea, and I planned it."

The man who was standing guard turned around. "Yeah, but we did a lot of the work, carrying those bags and putting them on the horses."

"You wouldn't have enough brains to pull off a job like this," the tall man said with a sneer.

"Yeah, you were real smart, Joe." The younger man looked at their leader with admiration in his expression. "Telling those people that someone would be watching to make sure they didn't move for fifteen minutes. They were so stupid they believed you!" He laughed.

The guard relaxed. "That was pretty smart, too, when you said you'd shoot the woman if the banker didn't cooperate. I guess you knew they'd do anything to protect her. How much was the haul?"

The younger robber looked down at the stacks of bills. "We're not finished counting it all, but there's more than one fortune here."

The guard whistled. "It's all right with me if Joe gets a larger cut. I could buy a ranch and run it for several years on my share, even if it is a smaller cut than he gets."

Frank's temper flared when the men talked about threatening Gerda. He had to take several deep breaths and force himself to remain coolheaded. He was a razor-sharp lawman. He wasn't going to make any mistakes this time.

With the guard not paying attention to what was going on around the camp, Frank knew it was time to attack. He signaled the other men. He watched them raise their guns and point them out between the trees. Then he stepped into the clearing.

"Drop your guns!" He used his most authoritative voice. "The members of a posse have their guns trained on you."

The guard dropped the rifle he was holding and raised his hands, and the young robber who was kneeling beside the money held up his hands, too.

"Take your pistols out of your holsters and throw them over here." Frank kept his steely tone.

The guard and the young robber complied, but the leader stood his ground.

"I don't believe you. There's only one of you and three of us." He pulled his gun and pointed it at Frank. "I can kill you before you get a shot off at any of us."

"Now!" Frank shouted.

The other six men stepped from the cover of the trees and underbrush. Each man was holding a rifle, all pointed at the bank robbers.

"I said drop your guns." Frank looked straight at the leader.

Venom accompanied the man's gaze. Frank suspected he wasn't used to having anyone get the drop on him. Slowly, the man lowered his arm, and his gun thudded to the ground.

Frank spoke to the posse. "Don't take your eyes off of the man you're covering, and if he pulls anything, shoot."

He walked to the leader and frisked him, finding another pistol hidden at his back under his belt and a knife in his boot. A woman's handbag was stuffed inside the man's shirt. Frank figured it was Gerda's. He glanced inside and hoped that all her money was still there.

"Weren't you going to share this with your gang?" Frank asked him.

A glare was the man's only answer to the question. After handcuffing the leader of the gang, Frank motioned Harold Jones over and stationed him beside the robber. Frank then searched the other two men. Neither of them had any hidden weapons, but the younger man had some bills stuffed inside his shirt.

"As the saying goes, there's no honor among thieves." Frank shook his head and ordered Harvey and Charlie Stevenson to guard these two robbers.

August took some rope and tied the captives' hands while Frank gathered up the money and stuffed it into the bank bags.

On the way back to town, the members of the posse were in high spirits. Even though they had to keep an eye on the prisoners, jubilant conversations bounced around the group.

When the ten men rode into town, a crowd quickly gathered. The sheriff met them outside his office.

"I see you caught them pretty quickly." He smiled up at Frank.

"We wouldn't have done it so soon if it hadn't been for August. He told us where to look." Frank didn't mind giving credit where it was due.

The sheriff turned toward August. "How did you know where to look?"

"When I realized which direction they went, I figured they might be where Pierre kept the girls."

The sheriff smiled as he and Frank helped the robbers dismount, then they herded the criminals into the jail cells and removed their bonds. The clang of the cell doors closing was music to Frank's ears.

The crowd outside the sheriff's office was growing. By the time the culprits were behind bars, almost everyone who was in town that day had gathered. The sheriff stepped out the door, followed by Frank.

Sheriff Bartlett raised his hands for silence. "Mr. Daggett led the posse that captured the robbers."

A shout went up. Frank's name and the word "hero" were among the shouts. Frank wanted to step back inside. He was just doing a job. He wasn't a hero.

August Nilsson moved to the front of the crowd and turned to face his friends. "Frank Daggett knew just how to take the men without anyone getting hurt. And we recovered all the money." He pointed to the moneybags hanging on the horses ridden by August, Hank, and Silas.

Gerda was standing at the edge of the crowd. Frank had seen her as soon as he'd stepped through the door. He watched the expressions on her face while the sheriff and August spoke. When she finally looked at him, admiration filled her solemn gaze. The connection he had felt that first day at the hotel once again sizzled through the air. The crowd faded away, and for a moment, he and Gerda were the only two people in the world. He slowly reached inside his shirt and extracted the woman's handbag he had stuffed there. He raised it, and her attention turned from him to what he held in his hand. She smiled and mouthed the words "thank you." For the first time in a long time, all was right with Frank's world.

ten

Gerda couldn't tear her gaze from Frank's compelling eyes, which were no longer icy but contained the blue warmth of a summer sky. She had a hard time catching her breath and suddenly felt warm all over. She hoped no one noticed that a blush now covered her cheeks. Or was it a flush? Blushes didn't usually make her feel this hot, and the temperature wasn't high enough today to bring on so much heat.

Her attention was drawn toward the sheriff, who was holding up his hands for silence. "Now seems like a good time to tell you all that I'm ready to retire. I've asked Frank Daggett to take my place." Murmurs through the crowd rose to a crescendo, almost drowning out his next words. "He hasn't said yes yet, but I'm hoping he will." The lawman turned and smiled at the man standing beside him.

The crowd clamored for Frank. Gerda glanced back toward him, and he still looked at her. Once again, she was held in his hypnotic stare. After an almost imperceptible nod, he turned his gaze from hers, and she watched him study the individuals who filled the street between them. A slow smile spread across his face, lighting his features. Then the chatter settled down as if the crowd was waiting for him to speak. Gerda wanted to hear what he would say, too. She knew he still hadn't invested in any business in town, even though that's what he'd said he wanted to do. He had purchased her dream house, but he hadn't moved in. There really was nothing to keep him in Litchfield, but now she didn't want him to leave.

"I've been thinking about Sheriff Bartlett's proposal." The rich tones of his voice carried over the crowd straight into Gerda's heart. "I really want to settle down here, and I've been a lawman all my life, so I've decided to take him up on his offer, if you good folks would have me as your sheriff."

The cheers drowned out anything else he might have been planning on saying. All Gerda could hear were the shouts and the loud drumbeat of her heart. But there was still a problem standing between them. Although Frank had been attending church, there was no indication that he had become a believer. Gerda couldn't see any future with the man unless he did, and it wouldn't be sincere if he only became a Christian because she wanted him to. It had to be for himself.

With turmoil churning inside her, Gerda slipped away from the crowd and headed back across the street toward the Dress Emporium. After what she had felt again today, she knew that the future sheriff of Litchfield tempted her. To protect her heart, she would just have to keep her distance. Gerda was glad that Frank was going to stay in town, and she was grateful to him for recovering her money, but she couldn't risk getting hurt. She had lived long enough to see how devastating a lost love could be for a woman. Olina had experienced it. So had Anna. And Gerda had been their friend through all the heartaches. She knew it wasn't something she wanted to endure. Especially not because of Frank Daggett.

When she arrived at the store, Gerda realized that she hadn't gotten the reticule with the money in it. With everyone still in the street gathered around Frank, she would just have to wait awhile. Once the crowd dispersed, she'd go over to the sheriff's office to retrieve it and then make her deposit. She headed into the back room to start working on the orders that needed to be completed this week.

శ

Frank saw Gerda slip away. What had gone wrong? He had felt such a connection with her—just like that first day in the hotel. Now she didn't seem to be interested in what was happening to him. Maybe she didn't want him to become sheriff. He needed to find out right away. It wasn't too late to change his mind. He might not look good in the eyes of the people around him if he withdrew his declaration, but it wasn't them he was trying to please.

He waved to the crowd and stepped off the boardwalk, heading toward the dress shop. When he went through the door, the bell tinkled. He glanced up at the brass clanger above the doorway before perusing every corner of the store. No one was in the shop. Gerda must have gone to the back room. Today, he was going to follow her. He took off his hat and held it in one hand, gently tapping it against his leg as he walked. When he parted the curtains, he had to duck his head a little to go between them. Gerda must have heard him enter, because she turned her startled gaze toward him.

"Mr. Daggett, what do you want?" Frank liked the breathless sound of her voice and the way her hand fluttered toward her throat. "Or should I say, Sheriff Daggett?"

Frank studied her for a moment before answering. A blush stole its way across her cheeks, giving them the look of fresh rose petals. Frank didn't know why he was thinking about flowers. It wasn't usual for him, but his feelings for Gerda caused everything in his life to turn upside down.

"Would you rather I didn't take the job as sheriff?"

Gerda took a quick breath before answering. "I think you'll

make a wonderful sheriff. And I want to thank you for getting my money back."

Frank remembered the woman's handbag he was still carrying. He gave it to her, then pulled his hat in front of him and started turning it around with both hands. "I was just doing my job."

Gerda's gaze dropped to the star on his chest. "You're already wearing the badge."

Frank tapped the metal with one finger. "The sheriff deputized me before I took the posse out. I forgot to give it back."

"I suppose you'll just exchange it for the sheriff's star, won't you?"

"If you think it's all right." It was important for Frank to hear her say that she wanted him to be sheriff.

"I, for one, would be glad to have you as our lawman. When would you start?" Gerda turned her attention to the reticule in her hands. Her fingers nervously plucked at it.

"I'm not sure. When I get back across the street, I'll ask Sheriff Bartlett when he wants me to start." He wanted to say something else, but he couldn't think of anything. "Good day, Gerda." Frank made his way through the curtains before he put his hat on his head. He was almost out the door before he heard Gerda's answer.

"Good day, Frank."

He liked the way his name sounded coming from her. Softly, he whistled a happy tune as he headed toward the sheriff's office.

&

The second week Frank was sheriff, he rode his horse all around town, checking for anything suspicious. This job might be the easiest he ever had. Everyone loved him and treated him as if he were someone special. After making a turn through the business section of town, he rode through the residential area across the railroad tracks, ending near the smithy and livery.

June had arrived the week before. It looked as if this summer wouldn't be as dry as last year when the livery burned down. This year, spring rains had nourished a good crop of wildflowers, which sprang up all over the place—in town and outside. Trees that dotted the landscape held abundant leaves in varying shades of lush green. Frank took a deep breath of the fresh-smelling air. A cool breeze kept him from getting hot on his ride. He could only think of one way that life could get any better, but he didn't want to torment himself with that remote possibility.

He took a quick glance around then dismounted his horse in front of the smithy. Maybe August would have time to visit with him. He entered the open door and was greeted by the smoky heat from the forge.

August was facing the door. "Frank, what brings you here? Did your horse throw another shoe?"

"No, I just thought I'd pay you a short visit—if you have the time."

August put down the tongs and mallet he was holding then wiped his hands on his large canvas apron. Then he pulled it over his head and laid it on the table beside his tools. "I'm ready for a break. Do you want to visit here or outside in the fresh air?"

"Outside would be fine."

The two men had just walked through the door when the stationmaster rode up. "I was glad to see your horse tied here, Sheriff Daggett. A rather large shipment arrived for you today. From somewhere back East."

Frank smiled. "It's probably my furniture."

"Yep," the stationmaster agreed. "Could be. There sure are lots of big crates. I thought you might need whatever it is right away, so I came to find you." ·

"I appreciate that. But there's no rush."

"I need to get back to the station. Good day, gents." The man wheeled his horse around and rode that direction.

"It sounds as though you're going to need that help we offered." August turned to look back toward a table along the wall of the smithy. "It's a good thing I don't have much left to do. I can complete it today."

"You don't have to help—"

"I was there when our family and friends offered to help you get your house ready. Everyone meant what they said."

"But they didn't know when my things would arrive. They might be busy right now—with planting and all that."

"That has been finished a long time." August looked at Frank with a shrewd expression on his face. "Don't you want us to help you?"

What could Frank say to that? Of course he wanted them to help, but he didn't want to be a bother. Then he remembered that Gerda was there when everyone agreed to help him, and she hadn't said that she wouldn't come. Any time he could spend with Gerda was good, wasn't it?

"When do you want to move your things?" August asked.

"I guess I need to clean the house up some, first."

"Today is Friday. I'll see if everyone can come early tomorrow morning. If all of us help, we can have the house ready for the furniture by tomorrow afternoon. I'm sure I can get my brother and brothers-in-law to help."

❧

August arrived at the Dress Emporium just before noon, carrying a picnic basket. Gerda was waiting on a customer in the shop when he came in, so he went into the workroom. When Gerda finished, she put the OUT TO LUNCH sign in the window and pulled down the shade on the door. Then she joined Anna and August. A wonderful meal was spread across the cutting table.

"We waited for you, Gerda." Anna turned from placing plates and napkins along the edge of the table. "August brought us a lunch from Mrs. Olson."

Gerda was glad that she wouldn't have to go up to her apartment to eat alone. Sometimes it seemed that everyone else had someone to share meals with. Of course she could go to either one of her brothers' houses for lunch, but she sometimes felt like a fifth wheel on a wagon when she did.

Gerda hugged her brother. "That was thoughtful of you."

They sat in the chairs that had been pulled close to the table. Then August said grace before Anna passed the food around.

When their plates were full, August started talking instead of eating. Gerda thought that was strange. August loved to eat. He worked hard, and he was a big man. He needed a lot of food to keep him going.

"I wanted to tell you something."

Wondering what it could be, Gerda put her fork down on her plate and waited with her hands clasped in her lap.

"Frank's furniture arrived on the morning train." August leaned forward as if eager to impart the news. "I thought it would be a good thing for all of us to help him tomorrow. I'll go talk to Gustaf and Lowell and Ollie."

Anna clasped her hands in her lap. "That will be so much fun. I've always wanted to see inside that house. If all the women get there early in the morning, we can have it cleaned up in plenty of time for the men to move in the furniture by afternoon."

August looked concerned. "I'm not sure about *all* the women. Several of you need to be careful." He glanced down at Anna's abdomen and blushed.

Anna patted his arm. "Oh, August, it won't hurt us to help Frank. Women have babies all the time, and it doesn't keep them from doing their work."

Gerda knew that it wouldn't be easy for her to go into that house and help clean it. The presence of Frank Daggett in the house she had dreamed of owning might be too much heartbreak for her.

"It might not be good to close the Dress Emporium tomorrow. People come into town on Saturdays, and often we get new business then." That sounded reasonable to her. "Maybe I should keep the store open."

"Nonsense." Anna was adamant. "I'll ask the Braxtons to keep an eye on things. If anyone needs us, they can come by Frank's house." She picked up a forkful of mashed potatoes and smiled at Gerda.

How could Gerda disagree with her?

When Marja came into the dress shop later that afternoon, Anna asked for her help.

"I'll come and work in the Dress Emporium, and Johan can run the mercantile." She clapped her hands as she usually did when she was excited. "That way we can help Sheriff Daggett and still keep both stores open." She wheeled around and started toward the door. "I'll go tell Johan. He'll be so glad we can be of assistance."

Now there was no reason for Gerda not to help. She even thought for a moment about feigning a headache or stomachache in the morning, but she knew that wouldn't be honest, so she resigned herself to being in her dream house most of the next day, with the man of her dreams—and both of them out of her reach.

>8<

The day turned out more festive than Frank had thought it would. Not only did the Nilssons and Jensons come to help get the house ready for him to move in, but also other people from the church arrived at various intervals during the first part of the morning. Soon the sound of hammers and saws filled the air as the men did minor repairs to the house that had sat vacant for almost a year. Some of the men even brought paint so they could help with the touch-up work. The women opened all the windows and swept and washed until everything in the house gleamed.

Right before noon, a wagon pulled up in front. Frank didn't have to wonder what the back of that wagon held. The tempting aromas of food wafted toward him, making his mouth water and his stomach growl. Belonging to a community satisfied something inside Frank and gave him something that he hadn't known he was lacking. It was almost unbelievable how much these people accepted him and loved him. Laughter and bantering conversations had rung throughout the house all morning. The only voice missing from all the happy noise was the one he most wanted to hear.

Gerda had been very quiet. She had worked efficiently, accomplishing a lot, but her quietness spoke more to his heart than all the loud chatter. Frank wondered if she was still upset because he had bought the house she planned to buy. He also wondered if there was anything he could do to take away the melancholy that surrounded her. It was odd to Frank that no one else noticed.

While Frank and August set up tables made of sawhorses and planks, the women bustled around and started bringing all kinds of food to cover them. Soon the workers gathered around the bounty, but no one ventured to pick up a plate to fill. For a moment Frank wondered why, then it hit him.

He turned toward the preacher, who looked more like a lumberjack that day since he was dressed in a plaid shirt and denim trousers. "Pastor Harrelson, would you say grace, so we can eat what these wonderful women prepared for us?"

Just before Frank bowed his head, he noticed that Gerda looked at him with a bemused expression on her face. He knew what grace was. His mother had always said a prayer before a meal when he was a young boy. Why should Gerda think he wouldn't know about that? Whenever he joined her family for a meal he always bowed his head when they said grace. That woman surely was a puzzle to him. A puzzle he wanted to solve really soon.

≈

After lunch, several of the men took their wagons to the station to pick up the crates of household furnishings. Gerda was glad they would be gone for a little while. All through the meal, she had felt Frank's gaze on her. She'd tried not to look directly at him, but occasionally she'd cast a sidelong glance his way. It was almost as if he were watching for her reaction to everything that happened today. How she wished she were back at the store, where she felt more comfortable doing what she usually did.

During the morning, Olina and Anna had tried to get her to participate in the discussions that went on all around. Although she answered their enquiries, she didn't feel like talking very much. The whole day had the feeling of a festival, but her heart wasn't in that kind of mood.

Although she'd never been inside it before, Gerda had fallen in love with the outside of the house. That's why she'd made inquiries about buying it. She knew that she could change how the inside was decorated if she needed to.

When she first walked into the parlor, she gasped. The wallpaper pattern was one of her favorites. Trellises, green leaves, and cabbage roses made the room feel like a garden. She knew just the kind of furniture she would use in it to make it feel like home.

Her fingers itched to make curtains to frame the windows with shades of fabric that would complement the wallpaper. If all this went on much longer, she might just have the headache or stomachache she'd thought about feigning yesterday.

When she finished in the parlor, she went to the dining room. Once again, the wallpaper pleased her, and she mentally placed a large cherrywood table in the center of the room. Carved lion's paw legs rested on a hand-loomed rug that echoed the wallpaper pattern.

She turned left at the doorway. Quickly, she toured the other rooms, upstairs and down. Everything she saw illustrated the home she hoped to have someday.

Soon the men returned from the station with their wagons loaded down with crates. Frank called Anna and Gerda into the parlor.

"I need a woman's touch to make this house a real home." He smiled at them. "Would you help me decide where to put the furniture?"

How could Gerda refuse graciously? There didn't seem to be any way.

When the men opened the first crate of furniture in the parlor, Gerda could hardly believe her eyes. The settee was the exact style she had imagined. Even the upholstery fabric was the same color. All she wanted to do was go home and spend time by herself. This day was one of the longest she had ever lived.

❧

When everyone had gone, Frank walked through his new house. It wasn't just a house. It looked like a real home. He was glad that he had asked Gerda and Anna to help him decide where to put each piece of furniture. There was something about a woman's perspective that added to each room's uniqueness.

Several of the other women had unpacked all the kitchen items while the furniture was being dispersed. It looked as if it was waiting for a cook to come and prepare a meal. The rest of the house was almost full. Of course, he would need to purchase a few items, but he wasn't in a hurry. He wanted Gerda to help him, but he knew she wasn't ready for that. She had been wonderful working with Anna and him today, but when it was time to leave, he felt her withdraw from him once again.

That woman was an enigma. Would he ever understand her?

eleven

Frank went to the hotel to check out of his room. He loaded his belongings on his horse and rode across town to his house—home. The word had a nice ring to it. It had been many years since he'd had a place to call home.

Frank took his horse into the small stable behind the house. While he groomed him, he familiarized himself with the rest of the structure.

His horse nudged him on the shoulder, trying to get his attention.

"You miss me talking to you, don't you?" He stroked the animal's glossy neck. "How would you like to share your home? I want to get a carriage. I won't ask you to pull it, my friend. There's plenty of room for another horse or two."

He finished grooming his stallion and gave him a scoop of oats. "Now that you've got your supper, I'm going in to enjoy the feast the women left in the kitchen for me. There's enough on the table and in the icebox to keep me from starving tonight and tomorrow."

When he arrived upstairs at the master bedroom, he dropped his saddlebags on top of the bureau. He'd unload them later. There were several boxes marked PERSONAL ITEMS sitting along one wall. Frank couldn't imagine what was in those boxes, but he would find out when he unpacked them. He decided to wait until after church tomorrow to do that. It had been a long day, and he was exhausted. All he wanted to do was try out the bathtub in the bathroom down the hall. A soak in hot water should help relieve the aches from all the activities his body wasn't used to. If he could talk to Mr. Nichols, he would thank him for installing one of those water heaters. Frank had loaded it with wood and lit it before he went to the hotel for his belongings.

He almost fell asleep in the tub, but when the water cooled, it brought him back to full awareness of his surroundings. After a late supper, he went right to bed. He didn't want to be late for the church service the next day.

Once again, this week's sermon made Frank think. Joseph Harrelson was a man of God, but he spoke to the lives of ordinary men—like a lawman who had drifted too long. He helped Frank understand that he needed an anchor, but Frank still didn't know how to find that anchor. He wished he had a Bible, so he could reread the verses the preacher shared with them. He wanted to mull over the words. Maybe on Monday he'd go to Braxton's Mercantile and see if they had any Bibles for sale.

After having lunch with August and Anna, Frank returned to his house, once again reveling in the joy of owning a home. The only thing that bothered him was the fact that he didn't have anyone to share his feelings with. *A man needed a wife in more ways than one.* Hard on the heels of that thought came the picture of Gerda as she helped arrange his house. She'd worn a scarf over her hair and tied it behind her neck. Tendrils crept out from under the covering, and she often blew them away from her face. Frank would like to see her in this house every day. Oh yes, she was just the woman this house needed. Although she had helped all day yesterday, she concentrated on the house and what needed to be done, instead of paying him any attention.

Frank took off his Sunday-go-to-meeting clothes and slid

into denim trousers and a well-worn plaid shirt. Today, he wasn't going to put on the star. He had a deputy who could take care of things this weekend. Once again, Frank's attention was drawn to the boxes by the wall in his bedroom. He might as well open them now.

When he took the lid off the first box, tears pooled in his eyes. There, carefully packed, were various sheets and pillowcases that his mother had lovingly decorated with colorful, embroidered flowers. When he was a lad, he had watched her work by the light of a kerosene lamp while rocking in her favorite chair. The warmth of those memories fueled the tears, and they poured down his cheeks unchecked. He placed the lid back on the box. He would probably use the linens, but he wasn't ready to unpack them yet. Here he was, a lawman who could face down the hardest criminal, blubbering over a few pieces of cloth. It was a good thing no one was watching.

The second box opened to reveal various items carefully wrapped in newspaper. He unwrapped one. It was a tiny shepherd girl made out of china. He remembered it sitting on a table by his mother's rocker. She often looked at it fondly. She said it was a touch of beauty in her life. Other beloved knickknacks of his mother's were also tucked into this box. He decided to store them in one of the bedrooms until he knew what he wanted to do with them. Later he might put a few of them on display in the parlor. They were fond reminders of his mother, and women seemed to like that sort of thing. Similar items were scattered about the parlors of the friends he had made here in Litchfield. Gerda and Anna had several of this style of knickknack on display in the Dress Emporium.

The last box he opened contained his mother's books. She

had always been a woman who loved to read. Some of the books, she had read to him. Adventure stories and tales about King Arthur and the Knights of the Round Table. He carried this box downstairs and started placing the books in the empty bookcase that had been set against a wall in the parlor. At the bottom of the box, Frank found his mother's Bible.

This was an answer to a prayer he hadn't even uttered. He had a Bible of his own. Frank thought for a minute until he called to mind the scripture reference Pastor Harrelson used this morning. Then he tried to find it. As he turned through the worn pages, there were many places where his mother had written notes in the margins, and all the family history was recorded on the parchment pages in the center of the book. Frank went to the rocking chair near the window—the one his mother had often sat in. He cradled the large book in his arms as he turned through each section. He knew he held a real treasure in his hands. His mother had been a godly woman. She knew what this book contained, and he vowed that he would, too—soon. Frank sat in the chair and read the verses from the morning sermon. Then he moved into other areas of the book. Before he realized it, the whole afternoon had passed, and the light was becoming too dim to read by.

❧

After spending Saturday at Frank's, Gerda's attraction to the man had multiplied. She pictured him in the house that was furnished much the way she would have done it. Thoughts of her and Frank sharing the home as man and wife tormented her. No matter how hard she tried to banish them, they crept back into her mind. *Oh, Father God, what am I going to do? Please help me get over my attraction to this man.*

Gerda again wished God would answer her audibly. She didn't care if it was thunder from heaven or just a whisper.

She just wanted God to tell her what to do. But her apartment was silent, and in the recesses of her mind where she often heard from God, silence also reigned.

On Monday, Gerda opened the store bright and early. She hoped that working on some of the orders for new clothes that were stacked up in the back room would give her something besides Frank Daggett to think about. She chose three different dresses she wanted to start working on today. She cut the dress lengths from the bolts of fabric the customers had chosen. Then she returned the rest of each bolt to the shelves behind the counter in the front of the store.

Gerda had just placed the last of the bolts on a shelf high above her head when she heard the bell above the door jingle. She turned to greet the customer but stopped in midstride. It wasn't a woman looking for something to wear who walked across the floor toward her. As if the thoughts she had been wrestling with had called him to come, the sheriff was striding toward her, his Stetson in hand, his boots beating a rhythm against the polished wooden floor. With each step, her heartbeat thudded just as loudly. The man looked too good in his black twill trousers and starched gray cotton shirt with the silver star shining on his chest. He had removed his hat, and dark curls tumbled across his brow framing his clear blue eyes. Even his mustache looked as if it had recently been trimmed.

"Well, do I pass inspection?" When Frank spoke, his voice tilted along with his upraised eyebrow.

Gerda gulped, and she felt a blush make its way to her cheeks. *I shouldn't have been staring at him.* She turned away and started rearranging the bolts that weren't in disarray. "What can I do for you, Sheriff?" She kept her head turned far enough that she could see what he was doing, even though her back was to him.

Frank set his Stetson down and leaned on the counter with both hands. "I thought I might be able to do something for you, Gerda."

She liked the way her name sounded coming from him. He always softened his rich, baritone voice when he spoke to her. Slowly, she turned and glanced up at him.

"I don't need any help, Frank."

His mesmerizing eyes held a twinkle. "I'm just making my rounds, checking on things. I'm glad everything's all right with you."

Gerda smiled. "Thank you."

"And I want to thank you for all the help you gave me on Saturday." The intensity of his gaze continued to hold her captive. "Without your suggestions, I probably would have lined the furniture up along the walls in each room. My house looks like a home thanks to you. . .and Anna."

Gerda thought the room had gradually gotten very warm. The intensity of the connection she felt to this man was almost tangible. *God, where are You now?*

Frank straightened. He picked up his hat from the counter and held it in front of his waist. "I'll be moseying on down the street. You be sure to get in touch with me if you need me for anything."

Gerda couldn't answer him. She just stood still and watched him walk out the door. When it latched behind him, she leaned back against the shelf behind her and took a deep breath. There seemed to be more air in the room now, and it felt cooler.

She went back into the workroom and sat in the chair by the window. She thought about every second that had transpired in the other room. Then she tried to shut Frank

Daggett out of her thoughts, but it didn't work. Maybe praying would help.

"Father God, I don't like what's happening to me. I want to be a wife and mother just as all my friends are. But I can't do that without a husband. Please, Lord, bring me a man to love. Surely You have one for me, and he won't be a man who doesn't profess to believe in You." She sat quietly for a few moments, then whispered, "Amen."

That evening when Gerda finished working, she returned to her apartment. She roamed the rooms restlessly and finally sat down and picked up her Bible. She reread the verses Pastor Joseph used yesterday. Once again, she agreed with what the pastor said. She was thankful God had provided such a strong man of God to share His Word with the congregation.

Gerda knew her problem was that she was alone. Everyone she knew had someone. Even former Sheriff Bartlett and Mrs. Jenson were getting married. She wanted a husband and family, and she didn't want to wait very long before she had them.

She leafed through the pages of her Bible. When her hands stilled, the book was open at First Corinthians. She began reading the words, trying to find some comfort. One verse almost leaped off the page at her.

She reread the words from chapter 10, verse 13.

There hath no temptation taken you but such as is common to man: but God is faithful, who will not suffer you to be tempted above that ye are able; but will with the temptation also make a way to escape, that ye may be able to bear it.

"That's what I'm trying to do, Lord." Gerda spoke the words aloud. "I want to escape from the temptation of Frank

Daggett. Father, he's not a believer, but he is such a temptation to me. Please give me a way to escape that temptation."

❧

Two days later, when Anna and Gerda were working together, Olina came to see them. The women had been chatting a few minutes when she said, "I have an idea. Why don't we give Frank a housewarming?"

"That would be wonderful!" Anna took the skirt she had been hemming and placed it on a worktable, then turned to look at her friends. "There are some things he still needs in his house."

Gerda wasn't sure it was such a good idea. It would mean spending more time with the man, and she was just now getting her emotions under control after his visit to the store on Monday.

Anna gestured toward her. "Don't you agree, Gerda?"

How could she not agree? If she didn't, they would both think she was awful. "It wouldn't hurt."

Anna looked at her as if she were crazy. "What a funny way to put it!"

Olina sat on one of the extra chairs. "I'm sure almost everyone will come to honor Frank. He's done so much for the town, and it'll be a way for people to show their appreciation."

Gerda thought that hiring him as sheriff had been a good way to show their appreciation, but she didn't say so.

"When should we have it?" Anna had picked up the tablet they kept in the workroom. She poised a pencil over it. "Do we want it to be a surprise to him, or should we tell him?"

"You know how men are." Olina laughed. "We'd better warn him, so his house won't be in disarray."

"Maybe we should ask him first." Gerda looked from one of her friends to the other. "He might not like it."

"What's not to like?" Anna asked. "But I think you're right. We should ask him what date he wants to do it, but we won't give him the option of not having one."

❧

Frank hadn't imagined anyone doing anything so wonderful for him. He thought they had assisted him more than enough when they'd helped him get his house ready and then move his furniture in. He'd almost told the women he didn't think this housewarming was necessary, but he was glad he hadn't. Gerda had been involved with it from the beginning, and now she was in his kitchen, looking as if she belonged there. Gerda, Anna, Olina, and the twins who had married Anna's brothers had cooked enough goodies to feed an army, and it was a good thing, because people had been coming by all afternoon.

Not only did they welcome him and share the refreshments, they all brought gifts. Frank was beginning to wonder what he was going to do with all the things they gave him. Some of the women had made lacy doilies to put on his furniture. Others brought things they had canned. He was glad to get all the jams and jellies. He really liked that stuff on his biscuits in the mornings. Many kinds of staples filled his pantry and overflowed onto the cabinets.

Frank wasn't sure why he needed all this food. He hadn't planned on doing a lot of cooking. He'd never really learned how to cook many things. He knew how to boil a pot of beans and fry a pan of corn bread. He could do a good breakfast—bacon or ham and eggs with biscuits. Or he could cook up a pan of mush, but for most of his other meals, he always went out. Maybe he would have to ask some of the women to teach him how to cook other things.

A couple of farmers had even brought hay and feed for his horse. He wouldn't have to buy anything for quite awhile.

August helped him stack the hay bales and sacks of feed in the stable.

"Thank you for all your help." Frank leaned his elbow on the top rail of one of the stalls. "I can't believe the bounty all you folks brought to me."

"That's how people around here are." August moved toward the open doorway. "I'm going to take the wagon home and come back with the buggy to pick up Anna. The springs are better on the buggy."

When the last of the visitors had left, Frank went to the kitchen. "Well, did they eat all the wonderful things you women fixed?"

Anna turned from the dishpan where her hands were busy with a dishrag in the sudsy water. "There are a few things left for you to eat." She nodded toward two plates piled high with cookies and pieces of cake.

Frank smiled at her. "Why don't you let me finish washing those dishes? You go sit down. You've been on your feet all day." He glanced toward the woman who was drying the dishes Anna had finished washing.

Anna looked as if she might object, but she stopped when she saw the direction he was looking. She quickly rinsed off her hands and dried them on one of the towels that had been in a package earlier that afternoon. "I do feel like resting a little. I think I'll try out that rocking chair until August gets here to pick me up." She stepped through the door toward the parlor.

Frank plunged his hands into the warm water and turned his attention toward Gerda. She had kept her distance ever since the Monday morning he'd visited her in the dress shop. He wanted that to change. At first she kept her gaze glued to the plate she was drying.

"Are you trying to rub the flowers off that dish? I don't

think they are supposed to come off." Frank chuckled at his own joke.

Gerda glanced toward him. She looked as if she were trying not to laugh. "That was really corny, Frank."

He rinsed another plate and handed it to her. When he did, their fingers brushed. For a moment, he thought she was going to drop the slick china. He grabbed for it, and his hands covered hers as they cradled the dish. She looked up at him, and the strong connection that sometimes came between them sizzled in the air. Frank could feel it, and the blue of her eyes darkened with intensity that held him captive. She gasped, and he felt her grip on the dish tighten, but she didn't look away.

They were standing so close he could see the golden tips at the end of her dark eyelashes. Wisps of blond curls around her face gave her a soft, vulnerable look. Frank wanted to pull her into his arms and place a kiss on the lips that were slightly open in surprise. Her gentle perfume filled his nostrils, and his heart longed for what he didn't have. Frank knew they were in dangerous territory, and he didn't want to frighten her, so he stepped back and released his hold on her hands. She took a deep breath and rubbed the moisture from the plate.

Frank started washing the other dishes. "It's been a wonderful afternoon, hasn't it?"

He sensed Gerda finally relaxing. He had done the right thing in stepping back, but it was one of the hardest things he had ever done. Never in his life had he wanted a woman more than he wanted this one. He remembered what he thought the first time he saw her. That she had strings hanging off her so long that they would really hog-tie a man. Well, he was a man who wanted to be hog-tied now, and he didn't think she was ready to hear that.

twelve

The rest of that week, Frank was eager to get home after work each day. He kept his mother's Bible on the table in the kitchen and read while he ate dinner. He couldn't get enough of it. He hadn't realized that the book contained so many interesting stories. When he read the words Jesus spoke in the New Testament, they tugged on his heart. If only Frank hadn't lived such a hard life. Maybe the words of Jesus could apply to his life, too.

The next Sunday at church, he sat where he could watch Gerda during the service. He always did that. He just couldn't get enough of looking at her. At first, he feasted on her loveliness. She was dressed in a shade of blue that matched her eyes. Although he couldn't see her eyes from where he sat, he knew that color would bring out the sparkle in them. She had her hair pulled up into a hairdo similar to the ones on those calendars that were becoming popular. The hat that rested on top of the pouf had a large, fluffy feather wound around the wide brim. Frank felt sure that feather would tickle any man who got near her. Maybe that was why she wore it.

Soon, Joseph Harrelson's words caught his attention and held it. Frank had learned to respect this man. Many of the preachers he had known in the past were either out of touch with the realities of life or they were complete hypocrites. Not Joseph. He lived the life he preached about, and he was keenly aware of what his parishioners were going through. They could see God in Pastor Harrelson's life. That was why the church services were always full. People loved Joseph, and they trusted him.

Frank leaned forward in his seat and hung onto every word the man spoke. Words of comfort for the grieving. Words of hope for those who were in despair. Then Joseph began telling about his own life.

"Before I came to know the Lord, I was a young, hot-headed gunman with a chip on my shoulder."

His words surprised Frank. He would have never guessed this about the man.

"I thought I was going to conquer the West with my lightning-fast guns. All I did was dig a deeper hole for my soul to sink into."

The preacher's words called out to Frank. He understood that kind of hole.

"I killed innocent men and misused women."

It seemed to Frank as if Joseph was talking about a stranger he once knew.

"I was finally arrested, convicted, and sent to prison. I thought it was the end of my life, but it was only the beginning. While I was there, a pastor visited me every day. He led me to the Lord and discipled me."

Frank wondered what that meant.

"Eventually, because of the change that had come about in my heart, God arranged for me to be set free from my life sentence. Only God could have accomplished that feat. After that, I couldn't do anything but preach the gospel of Jesus Christ. For the last five years, I've done that, and I've been in Litchfield for the last couple of years."

Frank was so engrossed in the sermon that he hadn't realized it was time for the service to be over. He was so deep in thought about what he'd heard that everyone had left the room without his knowing it, leaving him sitting on the pew. When Frank finally looked around, he was all alone in the house of God, wondering if maybe what Joseph had talked about could also happen to a man like himself. A man who had done more than his fair share of hard living. A man who had made his living with a gun—but on the right side of the law. A man who was ready for a change in his heart and life.

"God, I need some answers." He spoke the words aloud, not expecting an audible answer.

"Can we help?" The voice sounded familiar.

Frank turned to see Gustaf standing in the doorway with August right behind him.

"We wondered why you didn't come out of the building when everyone else did. We told the pastor that we'd check on you, so the Jensons wouldn't have to wait for Joseph to get to their house to start eating lunch." Gustaf dropped on the back pew beside Frank. "August and I sent our wives and family home together. We didn't want to leave you here alone if you needed us."

August stood behind his brother with one hand leaning on the end of pew. "We're here if you want to talk."

Frank was flabbergasted. In all of his adult life, he'd never had any friends like these two men. It was still hard for him to understand this kind of friendship. He rubbed his palms down his thighs while deciding what to say to them.

"I've been listening to the sermons and wondering what it's all about. I found my mother's Bible in the things I received last week, and I've been reading it." Frank wanted to stand up and pace, but he decided not to. "After the message today, I have a lot of questions."

August moved to the pew in front of where Frank and Gustaf sat. He dropped onto the seat but turned sideways in it so he could face Frank. "I'm not sure we'll know the answers, but you could ask us anyway. Maybe we can be of some help."

Now Frank couldn't stay seated. He stood and walked around the other end of the pew and along behind it. He leaned his hands on the back of the bench near where he had been sitting. There was something about this place that made him want to open his thoughts and heart to these friends.

"I've been hearing about Jesus and what He did to save people from their sins. I just have a hard time believing that all my sins can be forgiven." He straightened and rubbed the back of his neck with one hand. "It's only recently that I understood I needed this kind of thing."

Gustaf stood and faced him. "Everyone needs salvation."

August looked up at Frank. "A verse that comes to my mind is John 3:16 and the words that follow." He lifted an open Bible toward Frank. "They have been very important to me all my adult life. I've read them so many times, I can recite them. They're right there on that page if you want to follow along. 'For God so loved the world, that he gave His only begotten Son, that whosoever believeth in him should not perish, but have everlasting life. For God sent not his Son into the world to condemn the world; but that the world through him might be saved. He that believeth on him is not condemned: but he that believeth not is condemned already, because he hath not believed in the name of the only begotten Son of God.' You know, I believe that 'whosoever' means me. And it means you, too."

Gustaf added, "I've put my own name into that verse many times. For God so loved the world, that He gave His only begotten Son, that when Gustaf believes in Him, he shall not perish, but have everlasting life. It gives you a different perspective on it."

Frank could understand that. He read from the page before him. "For God so loved the world, that He gave His only begotten Son, that when Frank Daggett believes in Him, he shall not perish, but have everlasting life. I like the sound of that. But is it hard to live out?"

Gustaf gave a deep hearty laugh. "Life doesn't stop having problems just because you receive salvation from your sins. Life goes on, and you have to meet it head-on."

Frank moved back around the pew and sat beside Gustaf. "So tell me about your big problems."

"It's a long story, but I'll try to make it short." Gustaf leaned forward and dangled his hands between his knees. "When Olina came to the United States from Sweden, she was coming to marry our brother, Lars."

"I haven't met him, have I?" Frank leaned his arm along the back of the pew.

"No, he lives in Denver, and he doesn't come here very often."

Frank chuckled. "What terrible thing did he do to cause Olina to marry you instead?"

"He married another woman before she got here. Olina was devastated, and I didn't make it any better by not telling her right away when I met her at the docks in New York City. I really hadn't wanted to go meet her, but my parents asked me to. It was my plan to put her right back on a boat heading for Sweden. I didn't know that she'd gone against her father's wishes when she came here and she couldn't go back. It took awhile for it all to work out, but eventually we realized that it was God's plan for her to come here, and it wasn't to marry Lars. It was to marry me. God's thoughts and plans are often different from our own, but His way is always best." Gustaf leaned back in the pew and looked across at Frank. "When you have the Lord in your life, it's always easier to face major problems."

Then August turned toward Frank. "And if there is an area of your life that you haven't yielded to Him, it can cause you extreme difficulties. I resented Gustaf a lot of my younger life. I was jealous of him, and because of that jealousy, I almost missed the woman God intended for me to marry."

Frank squinted his eyes. "If I look confused, it's because I am. What are you talking about?"

Gustaf laughed. "I guess it's a lot to tell you all at once. I was keeping company with Anna before Olina came. After she arrived, I knew that because my thoughts were so often on Olina, I didn't love Anna the way she should be loved by a man who wanted to marry her. When I told her that we weren't right for each other, it broke her heart."

August took up the narrative. "I didn't want my brother's castoff. That's how I thought about Anna. It didn't matter that I had been interested in her long before my brother was but was too shy to say anything to her. After he was with her, I didn't want her, even though I did. Does that make any sense?"

Frank tried not to laugh. "I'm glad I'm not the only person who has had a mixed-up life."

"I waited around too long, and Olaf Johanson starting seeing Anna. They were engaged to be married."

This was getting interesting, almost like one of those dime novels Frank had read in the past. "So how did you get her away from him?"

August hung his head a minute before he raised it and continued. "Olaf was killed on a hunting trip right before the wedding. Anna was devastated. The funeral was on the day that was supposed to be their wedding. A lot happened, but eventually all of us listened to the Lord speaking to us, and Anna and I were married. But not until I had faced the jealousy that had consumed my life. The Lord helped Gustaf and me find the root of that jealousy and dig it out of my heart. Just think. If we hadn't listened to the Lord. . .or if we hadn't had Him in our lives, things might not have turned out they way they did."

Frank looked toward the one stained glass window behind the pulpit. The sun shining through the colored pieces of glass painted the room in a warm, multicolor glow. "I can see the need for having Him in my life. What do I do now?"

Gustaf stood and moved into the aisle between the pews. "We could go down to the altar at the front of the church. We'll kneel with you while you tell the Lord that you want Him to be a part of your life."

That sounded better than anything else he had heard that day. He wanted this salvation. He wanted what all the people he knew in Litchfield had in their lives, but he was afraid he wouldn't do it right. These friends could help him say the right thing.

August must have read his thoughts. "When you get down there, just tell Jesus that you know you're a sinner. You're sorry for all you've done, and you want Him to come into your life and change it."

That sounded simple enough. Frank hoped it would work with him. They knelt at the altar and he started speaking, hesitantly at first. Then the words poured out of him. Later, he wasn't sure exactly what all he'd said, but he did remember asking for forgiveness for his sins and telling Jesus that he wanted Him in his life from that point on. Tears were streaming down his face, and he didn't care that these two men were seeing them.

When the three men finally stood, Frank couldn't explain how he felt. It was as though he were a new man. One who hadn't done all the things that had affected his life. His heart was a clean slate, ready to receive whatever the Lord wanted to give him. And he felt lighter, as if a large burden had lifted from his mind and from his soul.

He looked at Gustaf. There was a hint of moisture around his eyes. He glanced at August, who had wet trails down his cheeks. These two friends had shed tears for him, and he loved them more than he had loved any other men he had ever known. A prayer of thanks for their friendship went up from his heart, and he knew that God heard every word of it.

When Frank arrived at home that afternoon, he started to change out of his good clothes. He opened the top drawer of his bureau. There, carelessly thrown aside, were his cigars and matches. He stared at them for a minute. He couldn't remember the last time he had lit one of the smelly things. None of his new friends smoked, and he hadn't wanted to do it around them. Now all desire for partaking in the use of tobacco had left him. Without hesitating, he picked up the cheroots and went downstairs to throw them away. He knew he would never smoke again.

thirteen

Soon after Gerda opened the Dress Emporium on Monday, Anna rushed through the door, carrying a basket over her arm.

"What's your hurry?" Gerda asked her. "You don't have to be here at a certain time. Actually, you don't have to come to work if you don't want to."

Anna set the basket down. The warm scent of cinnamon and fruit pastries quickly filled the workroom. "I brought you some apple fritters. I know how much you like them, and I'm sure you don't often take time to cook a good breakfast just for yourself."

Gerda knew her sheepish smile revealed the truth of that statement. "At least before I came down, I made a pot of tea to drink while I read my Bible this morning." She moved over to peer under the checkered napkin that covered the goodies. When she lifted the corner, steam escaped, bringing even more spicy fragrance with it. She took a deep breath of the heavenly scent and her stomach growled in a most unladylike manner. "I think I'll try one of these right now."

She went to the small cabinet that August had built into one corner of the workroom where she and Anna kept a supply of dishes and silverware on one shelf. She set a small plate on the table and lifted a warm fritter from the basket with a fork. She put it on the plate and cut a bite.

"Mmm, this is good." Gerda took her time enjoying the flavor. "Is my well-being the only reason you're here so early?"

Anna busied herself with one of the dresses they were

working on. "August suggested that I might want to get here early today." She ducked her head and concentrated hard on the skirt she was hemming.

Gerda put her fork down. "Now why would he do that?"

"I'm not sure, but he was in a good mood when he finally came home from church yesterday. That's all I know."

"Didn't he go home when you did?" Gerda sat in the chair by the window and took another bite. It tasted even better than the first one. If she ate like this every day, she would soon be unable to wear any of her clothes.

"No." Anna looked up. "I rode home with Olina and the children. August and Gustaf stayed to see about something. August came home after awhile with a twinkle in his eyes and a big smile on his face. I think he was even whistling a cheery tune. He doesn't often do that."

Soon the bell over the door in the front room jingled. Since Anna had her lap full with the skirt she was working on, Gerda went through the curtains separating the two rooms. Frank Daggett stood in the middle of the room, holding a large bouquet of flowers. It should have seemed incongruous for the masculine sheriff to have something so beautiful in his hands, but to Gerda, he looked wonderful. She wondered why he was there. And why he was carrying those fresh blossoms.

"Good morning, Gerda." His voice was soft as he said her name. It sounded like a caress.

"Sheriff." Gerda gave a slight nod, not able to take her eyes off him standing tall and regal. Just looking at him made her insides turn to jelly.

Something looked different about him this morning, but Gerda couldn't figure out what it was. He wasn't wearing his Stetson and his hands were full of flowers, but that shouldn't have made that much difference. As usual when he wasn't wearing a hat, curls fell across his forehead. Not for the first time, Gerda felt a strong desire to run her fingers through those dark locks. She took a deep breath. The expression in his blue eyes was warmer than she had ever seen it, but that wasn't enough to give her the feeling that something was drastically different. She just couldn't put her finger on what it was.

"Call me Frank, Gerda. I'm not wearing the star today." Then, as if he had just now realized what he was holding, he stepped closer to her and thrust the bouquet in her direction. "These are for you." He concentrated his attention on her face, almost as if he were trying to memorize every inch of it.

As she reached out to gather the flowers in her arms, Gerda felt a blush stain her cheeks. "Thank you. . .Frank." She buried her nose in the petals, savoring the scent of a summer meadow. "Let's go into the workroom. I have a vase we can put these in."

Frank pulled the curtains back for her then followed her into the next room.

When they entered, Anna looked up and smiled. "Why, Sheriff Daggett, it's good to see you this morning."

Gerda glanced back at Frank. He reached up as if to tip his hat, then dropped his hand back to his side because his hat wasn't there as it usually was. What was he doing here, and why did he bring her flowers? Gerda didn't get an answer to her question. Frank stayed for a few minutes and shared small talk with the two women, but he didn't say anything about his reason for being there.

Before he left, Gerda was once again captured by his gaze. Everything around them faded away. She allowed herself to get lost in the moment, but soon, he glanced toward the window.

"I need to get over to the office and relieve the deputy." Frank looked back toward Gerda. "I'll be seeing you soon. Gerda. . .Anna." He nodded at each woman before he exited the room.

Gerda stood where she was, lost in thought.

"Wasn't that nice of the sheriff to bring flowers?" Anna's words broke into Gerda's thoughts. "We should have offered him some of the fritters."

She looked toward Anna and gave her a distracted nod.

❧

Frank pinned on his star, then pushed the hair off his forehead and settled his Stetson on his head. He walked up one side of Main Street and down the other, then he crossed the tracks and strode toward the livery. Although it was late June, the temperature felt more like late spring than summer. A soft breeze blew through the trees, rustling the leaves. Birds chirped from among the branches, but he couldn't see any. He wondered just how many nests he would find if he were to climb some of those trees and search among the branches as he had done when he was a boy on the farm. The thought of a sheriff doing that brought a smile to his lips.

As he walked by one house, Frank caught the faint scent of the climbing roses on the trellis by the front porch. In other yards, various cultivated flowers added a multicolored patchwork to the manicured lawns. He couldn't ever remember noticing so many things about the landscape. Somehow, the earth felt new this morning. Maybe he should plant some roses or other flowers around his home. For a fleeting moment, he wondered if Gerda would like that. *I know she likes wildflowers.*

He reached the stable and looked inside. Hank was feeding some of the animals that were in the many stalls.

"Hank, is everything all right?"

The other man looked up. "Just fine, Sheriff."

Frank headed toward the smithy. The doors were wide open, so August must already be working.

When Frank darkened the doorway, August glanced toward him. "Ah, Frank, how are you this morning? Still feeling as good as you did yesterday?"

Frank took off his hat and gently tapped it on one leg while he talked. "Every bit as good. Does this feeling ever go away?"

August laughed. "It's really new to you. You'll get used to it, and some days you might not even notice, but the Lord's presence is always with you, and it changes everything in your life."

Frank stepped into the shaded interior of the building. August hadn't fired up the forge yet, so it was still comfortable.

"I took a big bouquet of those wildflowers you told me about to Gerda this morning."

Frank leaned against the table that ran along one wall of the smithy then placed his hat on a clear spot behind him.

August joined him. "How did that go?"

"All right, I guess. We just talked a few minutes, and I left."

"Did Anna offer you some of the apple fritters she made this morning?"

Suddenly, Frank realized that there had been a spicy fragrance in the workroom of the dress shop. He had concentrated on Gerda so much that he hadn't let it sink in. He chuckled.

"I didn't even notice them when I was there. I was. . .looking at Gerda."

August laughed hard. "You have it bad, don't you? Wait

until I tell Gustaf. He'll appreciate this."

Frank crossed his ankles and looked down at the toes of his boots. "I've never tried to woo a woman before. I'll try to remember all you and Gustaf told me about her. I just don't want to scare her away before I can ask her to marry me."

August laughed again.

Frank shook his head. "You sure are getting a lot of fun out of my predicament, August. Maybe it was a mistake to talk to you and Gustaf yesterday."

"No, Frank, we're glad you're interested in Gerda." He tried to smother another laugh and failed. "That's why we're going to help you with your courtship."

Frank tried to frown at him but didn't quite make it. "And I appreciate that. I just hope the flowers are a good enough hint."

When Frank walked away, his thoughts returned to his desire for a wife and children.

And not just any wife would do. It had to be Gerda Nilsson.

⋈

When Gerda went to her apartment for lunch, she couldn't get Frank out of her mind. The picture of the tall lawman standing in the middle of a women's dress shop, holding a bouquet of flowers, had set her heart beating almost double-time. She hadn't been able to settle down to anything for more than a few minutes the whole morning. Now, here she was trying to eat a light lunch, but the food didn't hold her interest either.

Gerda had set the bouquet on her dining room table. It took up too much space in the workroom. Besides, with it up here, maybe this afternoon she could concentrate on what needed to be done. She laid her fork on her plate and looked at the vase. She propped her elbows on the table—something her mother had told her never to do—then dropped her head into her hands.

Father God, I prayed for You to bring me a man to love. I asked You to remove the temptation of Frank Daggett, but You haven't. What am I supposed to do?

The food on her plate still didn't look appetizing. She took it over to the cabinet and covered it with a tea towel, then set it in the icebox. Maybe she would eat it for dinner.

Gerda paced through the dining room and into the parlor, then back again. The second time around, she stopped to look at the flowers. The only way Frank could have gotten a large bouquet like this was to pick them this morning. For some reason, she couldn't picture him out gathering wildflowers, but here they were—on her table. If he was going to go to that much trouble, why didn't he tell her why he'd brought them to her?

Soon Gerda returned to the dress shop. Anna was only working half a day today. She had gone home at lunchtime, so Gerda would be alone. Maybe she could get something accomplished this afternoon. She sat at the treadle sewing machine and looked out the window before she started sewing the seams on a light blue dimity dress for the mayor's daughter. Soon she was lost in getting as much of the sewing done as possible. She almost didn't hear the bell jingle when the shop door opened.

In a repeat of the morning, when Gerda went out front, Frank was standing in the middle of the room. This time, he held a small package. From the looks of it, she surmised he had probably wrapped it himself.

Gerda stood still and looked at him. "Do you need something, Frank?"

"Actually, I brought you something." He thrust the badly

wrapped package toward her.

She took it. "Why are you doing all this?"

Frank's gaze bored into hers with an expression that looked almost like yearning. "I'm really interested in you, Gerda." He reached his hand toward her before dropping it to his side.

Gerda glanced at the present in her hands. She moved to the counter and laid it down before she began opening it. The small box held a delicate china shepherdess. She gently picked it up and examined it. Anything to keep her attention off Frank. Because he wasn't a Christian, she didn't know what to say to his declaration.

"This is exquisite." She glanced up at the tall lawman who was studying her intently.

"It belonged to my mother." He blew out a deep breath. "I thought you might like to have it."

"I would, but maybe you should keep it in your family." She extended the figurine toward him.

"I don't have a family."

Such a mournful-sounding phrase.

Once again she was captured by his tender expression. What could she say? But she didn't want him to get the wrong impression.

"Frank, I don't know how to say this, but. . .you don't profess to be a believer. You are a good friend, but that's. . .all we can be." Her voice ended almost in a whisper.

If anything, his expression turned even more tender. "Gerda, I am a believer. I asked Jesus into my heart and life yesterday after church."

She studied his face. He seemed sincere, but could she trust appearances? What if he was just saying what he thought she would want to hear? "That's wonderful, Frank."

They stood and gazed at each other for another long moment. Then Frank dipped his head toward her. "I'll let you get back to work. I should as well."

With that, the lawman walked out the front door. Gerda stood staring after him, cradling the delicate figurine in her fingers.

What am I going to do, Lord? After this hurried prayer, Gerda went to the workroom to finish what she had started. She took the small china ornament and set it on the windowsill where she would see it from the sewing machine. After each seam, her attention was drawn to the gift. She stared at it for a few minutes before starting the next seam. *At this rate, I'll never finish the dress.*

Gerda looked at the watch that hung from the brooch on her blouse. It was getting late enough that she probably should close the store for the day. She was about to step through the curtains into the front room of the shop when the bell over the door jingled again. Her heart leaped then beat frantically. Her hand fluttered to her throat, trying to still her racing heartbeat. Was Frank back again? If so, what would he bring this time?

She pulled back one side of the curtains that covered the doorway, which revealed her brother August. She smiled at him and went to give him a hug.

"You seem a little jumpy today, Sister." His usually gruff voice sounded as though he was amused by something.

Gerda went behind the counter and leaned her forearms on the top. "No, I'm fine." She set the shepherdess she was carrying on the counter beside her.

"What's this?" The ornament was almost lost in August's huge hands. He turned it over and over and looked at it. "It's really pretty. Dainty, too."

Gerda couldn't take her gaze from the piece of porcelain. "Fra—Sheriff Daggett brought it to me this afternoon." She took it from her brother. "He said he's interested in me."

"And what do you think about that?" August stuffed his hands into the front pockets of his denim trousers.

"I think maybe he means romantically."

"I'm sure he does." August chuckled.

"I told him that I couldn't be interested in him more than just as friends, because he's not a believer in Jesus." Gerda set the porcelain girl on the counter again.

"What did he say to that?"

Gerda wondered why August was so interested. "He told me that he asked Jesus into his life yesterday. I hope he wasn't just saying that because he knew I would want to hear it."

August cleared his throat. "He wasn't. I was with him."

Gerda arched her brows, but before she could ask the question, August continued.

"Gustaf and I noticed that Frank hadn't come out of the church when everyone else did. We went to see if he needed any help."

Gerda was glad that her brothers were so observant.

"Frank had a lot of questions after Joseph's sermon. We answered them the best we could. After reading John 3:16, Frank wanted to ask Jesus into his life. Gustaf and I knelt at the altar with Frank and helped him pray to receive Jesus. I've never heard anyone more sincere than Frank was."

Tears pooled in Gerda's eyes. *That could change things*. Was it possible that Frank *was* the man God intended for her to have?

fourteen

The whole evening, Gerda couldn't get her conversation with her brother out of her mind. August didn't have any reason to lie to her, so she believed him. He was there when Frank knelt at the church altar and asked Jesus into his heart. So was Gustaf. Surely Frank didn't do it just to impress her. If so, why spend so much time asking questions about what Pastor Harrelson said? Besides, in his sermon on Sunday, Joseph had told about his life as a gunman before he gave his heart to Jesus. Frank had lived by the gun, too, but he hadn't broken the law. He upheld it. God could reach out to him just as well as he could reach into that prison to save Joseph Harrelson.

All the time Gerda dressed for bed, she thought about Frank. She brushed her hair one hundred strokes before plaiting it in a loose braid for sleep, remembering every expression on his face during each of his visits to the store that day. Looking at that tall man with a bouquet clutched in his masculine hands touched something deep inside her. Those hands were working hands—strong hands, bronzed by the sun, with fingers that could wield a hammer as well as a gun. She wondered how gentle those fingers would feel if they brushed her cheek.

Frank brought gifts to her and treated her with respect, even as his gaze seemed to devour her every expression. His eyes were like quicksilver, always changing. The blue going from light to a medium hue as he seemed to be memorizing her features. When his gaze connected with hers, his eyes were aflame with something that Gerda wasn't ready to put a name to.

She set her hairbrush down, walked over to her rocking chair, and picked up her Bible. When she sat down, it fell open in her lap at the first chapter of Job. Maybe his story of woe would take her mind off the puzzle that was Frank Daggett, handsome lawman and new Christian.

When she got to the eighth verse, she stopped.

Hast thou considered my servant Job, that there is none like him in the earth, a perfect and an upright man, one that feareth God, and escheweth evil?

These words fell into her heart. She remembered the day Anna brought her Bible to the shop and shared this verse with her. If God was bringing it to her attention more than once, maybe God saw Frank in a different way than Gerda had seen him all along. Maybe He saw the man Frank was going to become, not the one he had been. Maybe Frank was becoming an upright man who feared God and turned from evil. From what she knew, he certainly fought evil every chance he got.

Gerda bowed her head and closed her eyes. *Father God, are You trying to tell me something? I have begged You to take the temptation of Frank Daggett out of my life and heart, but he's still there. Now he knows You. Is he the man You prepared for me? Is he the reason I haven't felt drawn to any other man?*

She opened her eyes and lifted her head, then looked across the room at the empty settee. "God, I wish You were sitting there talking to me. I want to hear Your voice. I am so uncertain. Why does it have to be so hard to know for sure that I'm hearing from You?"

About midmorning on Tuesday, July 1, Frank went into the Dress Emporium. Gerda and a customer were looking at a stack of bolts on the counter. The colors of the fabrics ranged from indigo blue all the way through the colors of a rainbow and beyond. The woman seemed to be having a hard time deciding which to choose, so Frank walked around the store and looked at all the doodads sitting on shelves and furniture. Gerda or Anna had skillfully draped lacy things around them to display the items in an artistic manner. What was it about women that they could do that naturally? Frank knew he had never arranged anything to look that good. He pictured things lined up and in order, but usually they were boring to look at. That's why a man needed a woman to bring beauty into his life. A woman like Gerda.

When the customer finally went out the front door, Frank turned from where he was studying a display of gloves, handbags, and scarves. Gerda stood close behind him.

"Can I help you with anything, Frank?" The wary look that had been on her face yesterday was gone, and in its place was peace. Frank took that as a good sign.

"I came to ask you something, Gerda."

Her eyebrows lifted as if in question, but she didn't ask one.

"The picnic." Frank cleared his throat. She was so close that his nostrils filled with the delicate fragrance of some flower, but he wasn't sure what it was. Roses, maybe. He just knew that it came from Gerda. It drew him toward her like a bee to honey. He wanted to take her in his arms and bury his face in her abundant corn silk colored hair, but he held back. "Would you accompany me to the Independence Day picnic?"

Gerda stared into his eyes as if looking for something.

"That would be nice. I can make a basket of food to take."

"No need." Frank wanted to cradle her cheek in his hand. He was sure it would feel soft and smooth. Instead he stuffed both hands into his pockets. "I'll bring everything. All you have to do is get ready."

"Why, Frank." Gerda chuckled low in her throat. The sound caused a trembling in Frank's midsection. He had never had that happen before. "I didn't know that you could cook, too."

He laughed with her. "I wouldn't want the meal to be a disaster. Bacon or ham and eggs aren't right for a picnic. No, I'll have Mrs. Olson at the boardinghouse do the basket. I often eat there, and she's a good cook. She sure likes to mother the single men who frequent her place."

Gerda walked over to the counter, talking to him as she went, so he followed. "I didn't know you still ate there—since you moved into your house."

"It's easier than trying to cook for myself. As I said, my cooking abilities are limited."

She walked around the counter and reached behind it to lift something off the shelf. "I never thanked you for your gift." She held the figurine that had belonged to his mother in the palm of her hand. Her fingers caressed it as she talked. "I enjoy looking at her. I often put her near me when I'm working."

Frank leaned one hand on the counter. "Does she make you think of me, Gerda?" For some reason, the answer to this question was very important to him.

She didn't take her eyes off his and hers twinkled. "Oh, I don't need reminders to think of you." She must have realized how that sounded, because she looked down and blushed.

Frank smiled. That was the best thing anyone had ever

said to him. He was glad it was Gerda who'd said it. "Well, I'll come by your apartment at about ten o'clock on Friday."

"I'll be ready." Her whispered words reached him just before he went out the door.

౭

Gerda awoke early on Friday. Her stomach fluttered too much to eat any breakfast, so she just made a pot of tea. She took a leisurely bath and trimmed and buffed her nails until they had a healthy shine. After splashing on some rose water, she braided her hair and fastened it into a figure-eight bun at the nape of her neck. It took her a long time to decide what to wear. She tried on three different dresses before settling on a navy skirt and a crisp, white middy blouse with a sailor collar. The braid on the collar matched the color of the skirt. She liked the way the outfit emphasized her waist, and it wouldn't be too dressy for a picnic.

Gerda sat on the settee, listening to the traffic in the street. Too restless to stay seated, she went into her bedroom and peeked between the ruffled curtains. It looked as if everyone in town was headed in the direction of Lake Ripley. The people in Litchfield really liked to celebrate freedom. She glanced at the watch pinned to her collar. It was only 9:30.

When she sat in the rocking chair with a book of poetry, she didn't mind the wait. She enjoyed the rhythm and beauty of the words and the emotions they spoke about. Before she knew it, footsteps were coming up the wooden stairs. Gerda put down the book, looked at her watch again, and smiled. *Frank must have been eager, too. He's early.*

The knock was gentle but firm, just like Frank. Gerda opened the door. The man who stood there took her breath away. He was not the cowboy or the lawman. Frank was dressed in navy twill trousers and a navy-and-white-striped shirt. Without his hat, guns, and boots, he looked younger, more carefree. She liked what she saw.

"Gerda, you look wonderful." His eyes showed his appreciation.

"So do you." Gerda stood there for a minute, just looking at him. "Would you like to come in?"

Frank glanced past her. "I don't think that would be a good idea. You're here alone, aren't you?"

His thoughtfulness touched Gerda's heart. "Do we need one of my quilts to spread on the ground?" She turned to go get one.

"I brought one. Let's go down to the buggy."

Frank closed the door behind her and held her arm as they descended the stairs. The warmth of his touch spread up and down her arm, tingling as it went. When they rounded the corner of the store, Frank gestured toward a surrey with a fringed top. Its horse was tied to the hitching post.

"I haven't seen this buggy at the livery stable. Where did you rent it from?"

Frank helped her down from the boardwalk and up into the buggy. "It's mine, Gerda. I went to Minneapolis on Wednesday. It took me awhile to find just the one I wanted and the right horse to pull it. I drove it back yesterday." He untied the animal and climbed up on the seat beside her. "I couldn't take you places on my saddle horse, and I didn't want us to have to walk everywhere."

Gerda could hardly believe it. Frank had bought a buggy to take her places. The thought brought visions of being with him through all the seasons of the year—with autumn leaves falling, in the snow, when spring flowers were budding. . .

All the way to Lake Ripley, their conversation was light and refreshing, but she was constantly aware of the lithe man sharing the seat with her. His hands on the reins were skilled at controlling the horse, and muscles in his arms rippled as he moved with the action of the surrey. Occasionally, when the buggy hit a bump in the road, their shoulders touched. Each time it happened, Gerda's heart leaped. She hoped she wouldn't be breathless by the time they reached the picnic area.

The day was perfect. Although the sun shone brightly, it was cool under the trees where a gentle breeze blew across the lake. They spread their quilt near other members of her family. Soon everyone was visiting. At about eleven o'clock, the men decided to play a baseball game before lunch.

"I've never played before." Frank looked doubtful.

"That's all right." Gustaf clapped him on the shoulder. "We'll teach you."

Gerda was proud of Frank. It didn't take him long to get the hang of it, and he could hit the ball farther than any of the other men. As she watched him run and play, something inside Gerda melted. This man was amazing in every way.

Olina sat down beside Gerda. "I was surprised to see you come with Frank. Is he calling on you now?"

"This is the first time he has asked me to go anywhere with him." Gerda felt a blush creep over her cheeks.

Anna smiled. "I think it won't be the last."

I hope not. Gerda didn't dare say her thoughts aloud. She didn't want there to be too much talk about them.

Frank's team won the game. She was glad that her brothers were on his side.

The men jumped around as if they were boys. They clapped each other on the back and shouted.

"Playing baseball is hot work." Frank took his handkerchief from his back pocket and mopped his brow.

"Let's go wash up." Gustaf led the way to the stream that fed Lake Ripley.

The men washed their hands and faces in the cool, clear water. Gerda enjoyed watching the way Frank interacted with the others. He wasn't the sheriff today. He was just a man enjoying his friends, and it was a good thing. When the men returned to where the quilts were spread, water droplets decorated Frank's hair, looking like diamonds nestled in the curls.

The men had brought Pastor Joseph to eat with them. Before they said the blessing, Frank asked if he could tell them something. Gerda stood back and listened to every word he said. Each syllable sounded as if it came straight from his heart.

"I want to thank Joseph for the sermons he's been preaching, especially the one last Sunday." He nodded at the pastor. "And I want to thank August and Gustaf for taking the time after the service to answer all my questions. Because of these three men, I have accepted Jesus as the Lord of my life."

Everyone clapped and cheered. Other groups scattered around the lake looked at the ruckus, probably wondering what was going on.

After Joseph said a blessing for those gathered near, he sat on the quilt with Gerda and Frank. She was glad their pastor had joined them. The discussion centered on the Bible, and she enjoyed hearing what they talked about.

"Frank, have you thought about being baptized?" Joseph asked.

Frank put down the piece of fried chicken he was eating. He sat for a moment mulling it over.

"I think I'd like that."

"We could do it before we leave today. In Lake Ripley. The

water isn't too cold, and I wouldn't mind riding home in wet clothes. They would probably dry out pretty quickly."

Frank looked at Gerda as if asking her permission. She knew it wasn't her place to tell him what to do, but she wanted to let him know that it was fine with her. She gave him a slight nod.

"All right, Preacher, we're going to have a baptism today."

❧

As neighbors wandered from quilt to quilt, Frank relished the intervals when he and Gerda were by themselves. They shared stories of their childhoods and youths. The more he heard about Gerda, the more he loved her. He only hoped that the same was true for her.

As she talked, he watched the expressions that flitted across her face. She was so animated. He loved everything about her. The wind blew tendrils around her neck and face, and he wished that it would be appropriate for him to push them out of her way. He could imagine the feel of her silky hair in his fingers. One day, maybe it would be his right to touch her in such an intimate way. He could hardly wait.

About four o'clock, Joseph returned, bringing quite a crowd with him. He had found three more people who wanted to be a part of the baptism. Soon everyone who had scattered around the lake joined them on the side that held a small beach. The pastor took the four candidates for baptism to the edge of the water and decided what order they would go in. The sheriff would be last.

Frank watched as the man of God waded out into the water until it was up to his waist. Each person went to him, one at a time. He spoke solemn words over them then helped them bend over backward until they were completely under the surface of the lake. As they each came up out of the water, their faces beamed. When it was his turn, Frank went to his pastor and good friend. He listened to the words the man spoke over him and relaxed in his arms. When Frank came up out of the water, he knew that his face was shining, too. It was as if the symbolic baptism magnified the cleansing he had received when he accepted Jesus as his Savior. Some of the water streaming down his face wasn't from the lake.

Gerda stood on the bank holding his quilt ready to wrap him in it, but he didn't need it. He wanted to just drip dry.

"Why don't you put it on the wagon seat? That way, I won't get you wet as we drive home."

A heavenly melody was playing in his heart, and he knew it would continue until the day he died.

&

Frank often called on Gerda after the picnic. They spent time with her family or took walks in the evening or they drove through the countryside in the surrey. Every time they were together, they bonded on a deeper level. Gerda knew she didn't want to think about the possibility of Frank ever not being a part of her life.

Finally, one day, Frank put his arm around her when they were driving in the country. He pulled her against his side. Gerda thought she might faint from the wonderful way it felt to be so close to him. Every time he held her arm to help her across the street or her hand as they walked in the twilight, the connection had caused her to melt inside. But to be so close to him was heavenly. She sighed and nestled closer.

Although June and July had been cooler than usual, August was a scorcher. People were uncomfortable in the heat and disagreements often broke out, keeping Frank busier than usual. He even had to lock a couple of troublemakers in the jail, so he had to keep an eye on them. It had been a couple of days since Gerda had seen him, and she was missing their times together. Frank was becoming a necessity to her.

Gerda went into the mercantile to ask Marja Braxton a question. While she was there, a young man with low-slung guns came through the door. When Gerda first saw him, a shiver of apprehension coursed down her spine. Something wasn't right about this man. The two women watched him as he made his way around the store. He didn't really seem to be looking for anything in particular. Finally, he arrived where they were standing by the cash register. Because he made Gerda uncomfortable, she decided to go back to the dress shop. She could keep an eye on what was going on from there. When she turned to go, he pulled his guns and pointed one at her and one at Marja.

"You're not going anywhere." His harsh words brought Gerda back to stand near her friend.

"How much money do you have in that?" He nodded toward the register, never taking his eyes off of Marja and Gerda.

"Not very much." Gerda could tell from the sound of her voice that Marja was just as scared as she was. "We haven't been very busy today."

Gerda glanced at Marja, and she looked pale. Gerda inched closer to the older woman in case she fainted.

The gunman had to be in his teens, he looked so young. He pulled a dirty pillowcase from inside his shirt. "Put all the money in this." Then he shoved it toward Marja.

Marja was shaking so badly, Gerda didn't think she would be able to move. "I'll do it for you," she whispered to her friend. Marja nodded, and Gerda took the bag from his hand.

She opened the drawer and removed the bills from each

compartment, stuffing them in the case. Then she scooped up the coins and put them into the bag. She tied a loose knot in the end to keep the money from coming out. She didn't want anything to upset the man. He might shoot one of them. He took the bag and stuffed it back inside his shirt. Now it wasn't as flat as it had been when he came in. Through his shirt, it looked like a tumor on his stomach. Gerda almost giggled at that thought, but she knew it was because she was close to becoming hysterical.

"Lay facedown on the floor." His words sounded harsh.

Gerda was getting tired of this. She hadn't seen a robbery in all her life until this year. Now she had experienced two. She got as close as she could to Marja and slid her hand over to clasp Marja's icy one. They heard the robber clomp to the door.

⋙

Frank was sitting in his office, thinking about Gerda. One day soon, he was going to ask her to marry him, but he wanted to plan the right time to do it. It had to be perfect. . .for her.

Hank from the livery ran to the door of his office. "Come quick, Sheriff! Someone's robbing the mercantile!" The man was so excited his voice trembled, and he was almost gasping for breath.

Frank jumped up and grabbed his guns. "How many men? I didn't hear a gang ride into town."

"It wasn't no gang." Hank hurried along with Frank as he went toward the store. "I was just going in when I noticed a man in the back holding his guns on Marja and Gerda. I ran over here as fast as I could."

Frank's heart dropped to his toes when he thought about a man holding a gun on Gerda again. For a moment, red-hot anger swelled within him. Then reason returned. Frank was a lawman. He had to think rationally. Besides, he didn't think a Christian should be having such hateful thoughts. This was the hardest thing he'd had to face since becoming a believer.

Why had he taken so long to get around to asking Gerda to marry him? He hadn't wanted to rush her, but what if the man's trigger finger got itchy? He might shoot either one of the women with very little provocation. Frank hoped he'd get there in time to avert a tragedy.

❧

When the man ran through the door, Gerda got up and rushed to look out the windows at the front of the building. She got there just in time to see the gunman run straight into Frank. The two men crashed to the boardwalk in a tangle of arms and legs. In the struggle to get free from the mess, the thief's pistol fired, even though he seemed to be trying to shove it into his holster. Frank went still. The kid jumped up and sprinted across the street. Hank and the stationmaster tackled him before he reached his horse. They held him and looked back toward the boardwalk.

She could hardly believe her eyes. Frank was lying in a pool of blood. She ran to him and dropped to her knees, frantically feeling for his pulse. At least it was strong.

Gerda shouted to Hank. "Please! Go get Dr. Bradley!" The pool of blood didn't seem to be getting any larger, and Gerda was afraid she would hurt him if she tried to move him. Then she began to weep over the man she loved with all her heart.

❧

Frank could hardly believe it. That juvenile robber shot him while he was trying to catch hold of him. His shoulder felt like it was on fire. He gritted his teeth and shut his eyes. Before he opened them again, Gerda had dropped to the boardwalk beside him and she was yelling for someone to get the doctor. He relaxed and kept his eyes shut. There was nothing else he could do until the doctor got there.

Gerda's hot tears began falling onto his face, and she started praying for him. Her prayer warmed his heart.

"Oh, God. I love Frank and can't live without him. Please make sure he stays alive."

Oh, he was alive all right. He hurt a lot, but he was alive and aware of every word she said.

Frank slowly opened his eyes and gazed into Gerda's troubled face. "Gerda, will you marry me?"

She looked startled, but she nodded just before Doc took her place beside him.

fifteen

You're lucky, Sheriff," the doctor said as he finished bandaging Frank's shoulder. "It's just a flesh wound. It bled a lot, but it wasn't that bad." He started putting his supplies back into the cabinet.

"Thanks, Doc." Frank grimaced. "It hurts, even if it is a flesh wound."

The doctor walked back toward him and grinned. "I didn't say it wouldn't hurt. I just meant it's not as bad as it could have been if it had torn the muscle or hit a bone."

Frank started to stand up so he could put on his shirt.

"Stay seated, Sheriff," Doc said as he helped Frank ease the shirt over his shoulder. "You might want to be careful for the first week. Give it time to heal." Dr. Bradley picked up a large square of white cloth. "You should wear this sling for at least that long."

He folded the cloth into a triangle and tied the ends around Frank's neck. Then he helped slide Frank's arm into the fold. It did take some of the pressure off the wound.

"I'll give you some laudanum to take for the pain. Wait until you get home then put a few drops in a glass of water. It'll help you sleep." The doctor handed Frank a small, brown glass bottle with a cork in the top. "While you sleep, your body will begin to heal. The longer you stay up fighting the pain, the longer it'll take."

Doc walked over and glanced into his waiting room. "Are one of these men going to take you home?"

August must have been watching, because he quickly came to the door. "I'll take him."

"He doesn't need to ride a horse right now."

Frank tried to smile at them. He wasn't sure it worked. "I didn't ride my horse to the office today. I walked."

"I'll go get your buggy. It has the best springs of any in town. It should ride smooth enough if we take it slow." August quickly went out the door.

Frank was glad when they got up the stairs in his house. August helped him out of his clothes and into bed. Then he went downstairs to get a glass of water for the laudanum. While he was gone, Frank tried to ignore the excruciating pain burning in his shoulder by thinking about Gerda. He couldn't believe he had blurted those words to her out in the street. She deserved better than that. Besides, he really wanted to tell her how he had fallen in love with her over the time he had been in Litchfield. She needed to hear all of it. When he was better, he would rectify that.

❧

All Gerda thought about that afternoon were Frank's last words to her. She wondered if he knew what he had said. He had been shot, and he had lost quite a bit of blood. Besides, he had to be in a lot of pain. Maybe he was out of his head. She wanted to see him so she could know whether he meant it.

When it was almost evening, Anna came to see Gerda.

"August told me that Doc said Frank needed strong beef broth today. I've made some. Would you like to go with me when I take it to him?"

Tears rolled down Gerda's cheeks, and she hugged Anna. "Thank you. I wanted to see how he is doing, but I knew I couldn't go see him alone."

August met Gerda and Anna at the house. He went up to

check on Frank while the women put the pot of broth on the stove to heat it some. It shouldn't be too hot for Frank to drink, but it needed to be warm. Gerda was surprised to see how clean and neat everything was. She knew how messy her brothers had always been. If they lived alone in a house, she was sure it would have looked messy most of the time. Maybe Frank paid someone to clean for him. She hadn't heard anyone say they were doing it, but surely a man wasn't this neat. There weren't even any dirty dishes in the sink. She would have expected him to leave his breakfast dishes until later in the day. Maybe she didn't know Frank as well as she thought she did.

August came downstairs. "You can take the broth up to Frank now."

Anna picked up a tray with a mug of the steaming liquid on it. Gerda followed her, carrying a napkin. August accompanied them back upstairs. He went in the bedroom first and helped Frank sit up against his pillows.

When August opened the door again, Gerda and Anna entered. Frank looked pale and his eyes were glassy. Gerda tucked the napkin into the neck of his shirt. When the back of her fingers brushed against the warm flesh of his throat, her hands trembled. To be so close to him—and he was so drowsy he didn't even seem to know who was ministering to his needs. Anna set the tray down and went toward the door.

"Where are you going?" August put his arm around his wife.

"I think we'll need to spoon the broth into his mouth. He won't be able to hold the mug and drink."

"I'll go." He dropped a quick kiss on her forehead and glanced down at her abdomen, which was beginning to protrude. "You just wait up here."

A pain shot through Gerda's heart at this display of affection.

She wanted to be married, and Frank had even asked her, but she still didn't know if he was aware of doing so.

❧

The next day, several people came to check on Frank and bring him something to eat. He sort of remembered Gerda being here the first day, but he wasn't sure. The laudanum really clouded his mind. He hoped he hadn't done or said anything to offend her, because he was pretty sure she hadn't returned. Of course, many people in town wanted to help him. Someone probably worked out a schedule, to keep them from all coming at once.

By evening, Frank decided not to take any more laudanum. The pain had lessened some, and he would rather be able to think straight, even if he hurt. Mrs. Olson came the next morning. Frank was thankful she'd brought a more substantial meal for breakfast. He would never gain the strength he needed if all he did was eat broth and soup. The bacon with scrambled eggs and hot biscuits were the best he had ever tasted. Of course, it could be just because he hadn't had any real solid food since he was shot.

After Mrs. Olson left, Frank got up and dressed himself. He took his time, and although it hurt, he was able to slip into his clothes and boots. He didn't mind putting the sling back on when he was finished. His shoulder needed relief from the pressure. He made his way down the stairs and out to the stable. He planned to feed the horses, but they were already munching on grain when he went into the building.

"Whom should I thank for that?" he whispered as he rubbed the saddle horse's neck.

He stepped back outside. The morning air was pure and fresh, and he filled his lungs with a large breath. It was a bright, sunny day, but it hadn't gotten too hot yet. In the trees above him, Frank could hear birds chattering as they hopped from branch to branch. The two kinds of chirping suggested there were baby birds in a nest up there. It gave him a good feeling, so he decided to try to take a walk. He could always turn back if he needed to.

After going a couple of blocks, he circled around to the other side and made a complete loop back to his house. Although he felt a little tired, he knew it wouldn't take him long to regain his strength. He was determined that this wound wouldn't keep him down.

The next morning, Frank went all the way to his office. He moved slowly as he stepped up onto the boardwalk before opening the door.

"What are you doing here, Sheriff?" Deputy Clarence Wright got up from his chair so fast it almost fell over. "I didn't expect you for several more days."

Frank smiled. "Just thought I'd check and see if everything is all right." He sat at his desk and sorted through the papers on top.

When he got up, he went back to the cell where the young man who shot him was being held. "Where you from, young man?"

The scruffy man turned away from Frank. He clenched the bars in the window so tight that his knuckles turned white. He was just a kid.

"What's your name?" Frank waited awhile for an answer that never came.

Frank walked back into his office. "What's being done for the prisoner?"

"I'm making sure he is fed." Clarence glanced back toward the belligerent youth. "My wife fixes extra, so I know it's good food."

Frank nodded. "I'm sure it is."

"I've wired the U.S. Marshals to see if the kid is a known criminal."

"Did he tell you his name?"

"Naw. I just used a description." Clarence shoved his hands into his back pockets.

Frank reached for the doorknob and nodded. "You're doing a good job, Deputy."

Frank crossed the street and headed toward the Dress Emporium. No one was in the front room, but the curtains parted immediately after he closed the door behind himself.

"Frank! What are you doing here?" Gerda's voice sounded breathless.

He smiled. "I couldn't wait any longer to come see you." For a moment he studied her face, drinking in the appearance of her creamy complexion, corn silk colored hair, and full, red lips.

An expectant look dropped into Gerda's blue eyes. She seemed to be waiting for something.

"I wanted to ask if you would let me take you to dinner tonight. . .at the hotel."

Her expression changed to one of concern. "Are you sure you should be out yet?"

Frank walked over and leaned his good hand on the counter. "Gerda, I'm a strong, healthy man. It doesn't take that long for me to heal. I don't want to just lie in bed. It'll make me weaker."

A smile lit Gerda's face. "I'd love to go to dinner with you, Frank."

◆

Gerda closed the shop a little early and went to her apartment to get ready. She wanted to look her best tonight. She just hoped that Frank wasn't overdoing it. When he said he was a strong, healthy man, she'd wholeheartedly agreed with him—in her mind. It was hard to believe that the man was wounded. He was an imposing presence in the midst of all the feminine wares in her shop. He wasn't wearing a hat, so his curls were a riot framing his handsome face. His eyes were bright and clear, and the sling didn't detract from his virility.

Surely there was a special reason he wanted them to go out tonight. Maybe he was going to say something about his proposal. Or maybe he was going to tell her that he had been delirious. That thought caused Gerda to stop and sit down. *Please, God, don't let him be sorry for what he said. I don't think I could take it if he is. Please let him be the man You want for me.* What a change from all those months she'd prayed to be freed from the temptation he presented! Now she was asking God to keep him in her life.

Gerda had just finished putting her hair up in a new, soft style when a knock sounded on the door. She patted her coiffure and took one more look in the cheval glass. She was pleased with her reflection.

"Frank." When she opened the door, she had to hold on to it to keep from trembling. Tonight, he looked devastatingly masculine. His muscles filled out his shirt in a wonderful way.

He continued to stand on the landing outside the door. "If you're ready, we can go."

When they arrived at the restaurant in the hotel, Frank asked to be seated as far away as possible from the other diners. After Molly took their orders, he reached across the table with his good hand and took one of Gerda's. He gently rubbed his thumb across her fingers, and a sparkling sensation shot up her arm straight to her heart. As their clasped hands rested on the white linen tablecloth, they sat and gazed at each other. Gerda felt the same strength of connection she had felt that first day in the hotel lobby. What was it about this man that he had that kind of effect on her?

"Dear, dear Gerda," Frank said in a husky whisper. "I must tell you what I feel for you."

With each word, Gerda's pulse accelerated until she was sure her heart would jump out of her chest. Breathlessly, she waited for him to continue.

"I'm sorry I blurted those words in the street."

Gerda felt as if she had slammed against a wall. She dropped her gaze to their hands and started to pull away, but he held her fingers in a tight grip.

"I'm not sorry for the words, just for the time and place. I was frightened for you when I heard that robber had a gun on you. I felt I had waited too long to express my love to you."

Gerda raised her eyes and saw love radiating from his face.

"I've felt a strong connection with you since the first time I laid eyes on you. I believe you felt it, too."

She nodded. "It scared me." She could barely get the words out past the anticipation that had invaded her entire being.

He chuckled. "Me, too. I didn't understand it. It was more than just a physical attraction. Oh, don't get me wrong. I saw how beautiful and desirable you were."

Gerda felt a blush stain her cheeks. She ducked her head.

"Look at me, Gerda." Frank's expression was earnest. "I didn't really understand the connection until after I accepted Jesus into my heart. I believe that God saved you for me. He knew that the best way He could reach me was for me to stay here and become a part of this town. I learned from you and all our friends the truth as it was lived out every day. If I hadn't felt that connection with you, I would have moved on. It was part of God's great plan for my life."

Gerda could believe that. "All my close friends and family had someone special, and I had been praying for God to bring me a man to love. Although I felt the connection to you, I knew you weren't the man He would want me to marry. I even thought that you said you'd accepted Jesus just because you knew I wanted to hear it. I'm sorry for that."

Frank smiled. "What made you change your mind?"

"August told me about the Sunday you talked to him and Gustaf. I knew you wouldn't have asked all those questions if you were just doing it for me. I recognized that it was real."

The waitress came with their food, so Frank let go of Gerda's fingers. He couldn't eat with one arm in a sling and the other holding her hand.

They savored a portion of their tender roast beef, potatoes, gravy, and hot buttered rolls, but soon they continued their discussion.

"What I feel goes way beyond the physical. I believe that God created us for each other."

Gerda nodded her agreement.

"I felt my love for you grow every time I saw you. You were an honest, godly woman in every situation. I saw how you treated everyone you came in contact with. When I bought that house, even before I knew you had wanted it, I dreamed of you sharing it with me. . .as my wife. I can't imagine any other woman in my life."

Gerda put her fork down on her plate and rested her hands in her lap. "I must confess that I prayed earnestly for God to remove you from my life because you were such a temptation. I would never marry an unbeliever, but you were never far from my thoughts. That's why I tried so hard not to be around you. Did you know that I was hesitant when the rest of my family wanted to help you?"

Frank laughed and laid his good hand on the table. "It's funny, but it was as if I could sense so much about you. I knew, and I wondered about it. Little did I know that you felt I was a temptation."

Gerda reached across and touched his hand. "That first night after I saw you in the hotel, I dreamed about you."

Frank turned his palm up under her hand and gripped it. "I dreamed about you, too. You were waiting for me to come home. When I woke up, the dream disturbed me so much that I couldn't go back to sleep. I didn't think I had anything to offer a woman like you, and I really didn't at the time. But now I do. Gerda, will you marry me and share my home. . . and be the mother of my children?"

His proposal took her breath away. The images it brought to mind flooded her whole body with heat. Gerda wondered if he could feel it through her hand. She couldn't take her eyes from his intense gaze. She welcomed the love pouring from him into her heart, and she hoped he could feel hers radiating to him. The sound of voices and silverware against china faded away, and it was as though they were the only two people on earth. For a moment, Gerda felt as if the windows of heaven had opened and God was pouring His blessing on their relationship.

"I love you so much." Frank's words penetrated her heart. "And I will love you until the day I die. Please don't make me wait too long for the wedding."

Gerda gave a soft laugh. "Why, Frank, how could I?"

❧

When they had finished eating, Frank wanted to get Gerda alone, but he also wanted to protect her reputation. "Do you feel like a stroll this evening?" He eased her chair back as she arose from the table.

She looked up at him. A smile gave a gentle glow to her face. "Of course, the evening is beautiful."

He wondered how she could know that, since she hadn't even glanced out the window the whole time they were in the restaurant. Maybe she felt the same way he did—that all was right with the world now that they had defined their relationship.

As they walked along, talking about nothing and everything, Frank was oblivious to everything but the beautiful woman by his side—the woman who would soon be his wife. He hadn't planned to go anywhere in particular, but he wasn't surprised when they arrived at his house—soon to become their home.

Frank was glad he had hung a porch swing near the trellis he'd built for the climbing roses he'd planted earlier. They weren't very tall, they were already blooming. Every morning the fragrance of those roses, touched with dew, reminded him of Gerda. Although it would cause tongues to wag if they went inside the house, he knew they could sit on the porch and talk as twilight deepened.

Once they were seated in the swing, Frank reached into his coat pocket. He pulled out a velvet pouch and handed it to Gerda. "The first time I saw you, your delicate features made me think about this cameo. It belonged to my mother. I hoped the day would come that I could give it to you because you were going to become my wife."

"Thank you, Frank." Gerda opened the pouch and slid the brooch into her hand. The gold filigree that framed the stone gave it a delicate design. "I will wear it on our wedding day."

Frank gently rocked the swing with one foot. "How long do you need to plan a wedding?"

"Well, I'm sure all my family and friends will want to help." Gerda smiled up at him making his heart beat double-time.

He didn't want to wait any longer than necessary for the wedding. "Are you going to make me wait a long time?"

Gerda ducked her head. "No, Frank. I'm as anxious as you are."

Even in the waning light of day, Frank could see the blush that stained her cheeks. "Can you be ready in a month?"

Gerda nodded and looked into his eyes. "How does the last Saturday in September sound to you?"

"Just fine." He slid his arm around her shoulders and pulled her close into his embrace.

By the time they arrived at that decision, twilight had disappeared, and the summer night sky sparkled with a million bright stars. Frank was glad the moon was shining from the other side of the porch, casting the two of them into the shadows. He felt as if he had wanted to kiss Gerda all his life. Now the time had come, and he wanted her to experience all his love for her, wrapped up in that kiss.

☙

When Frank pulled her against his side with his good arm, Gerda knew what was going to happen, and she welcomed it. She turned her face up toward his. In the shadows, his eyes shone brightly. She gazed into them, and her throat went dry. Without thinking, she moistened her lips as his face drifted toward hers. She closed her eyes so she could savor every nuance of her first kiss. When his lips gently touched each of her eyelids, she felt tears pool under each lid at his tenderness. As his lips feathered across her cheeks, his soft mustache tickled in a most delicious way. The anticipation building inside her made her feel as if she might explode with delirious happiness.

Finally, his lips touched hers tentatively as though he wanted her to become familiar with the shape of them. His wonderful mouth finally settled firmly on hers. When the kiss eventually deepened, Gerda felt as if their very essence mingled in an indefinable way. She gave herself up to the kiss, pouring all her love for this man into it.

When their lips parted, Gerda gazed into the face of her beloved. "I'm glad God sent a lawman to capture my heart," she whispered.

Frank pulled her closer and settled his chin against her hair. "I am, too, Gerda. I am, too."

A Letter To Our Readers

Dear Reader:

In order that we might better contribute to your reading enjoyment, we would appreciate your taking a few minutes to respond to the following questions. We welcome your comments and read each form and letter we receive. When completed, please return to the following:

Fiction Editor
Heartsong Presents
PO Box 719
Uhrichsville, Ohio 44683

1. Did you enjoy reading *Gerda's Lawman* by Lena Nelson Dooley?
   ❑ Very much! I would like to see more books by this author!
   ❑ Moderately. I would have enjoyed it more if

   _____

   _____

   _____

2. Are you a member of **Heartsong Presents**? ❑ Yes ❑ No
   If no, where did you purchase this book? _____

   _____

3. How would you rate, on a scale from 1 (poor) to 5 (superior), the cover design? _____

4. On a scale from 1 (poor) to 10 (superior), please rate the following elements.

   ____ Heroine   ____ Plot
   ____ Hero   ____ Inspirational theme
   ____ Setting   ____ Secondary characters

5. These characters were special because?_____

_____

_____

6. How has this book inspired your life?_____

_____

_____

7. What settings would you like to see covered in future
   Heartsong Presents books? _____

_____

_____

8. What are some inspirational themes you would like to see
   treated in future books? _____

_____

_____

9. Would you be interested in reading other **Heartsong
   Presents** titles? ❑ Yes ❑ No

10. Please check your age range:
   ❑ Under 18   ❑ 18-24
   ❑ 25-34   ❑ 35-45
   ❑ 46-55   ❑ Over 55

Name _____

Occupation _____

Address _____

City_____ State_____ Zip_____

The STUFF OF LOVE

4 stories in 1

In four interwoven novellas set in 1941, an American OSS officer enlists a mother and daughter in America and two of their relatives in Europe to carry out a clever plan.

The southern California mother/daughter team of Cathy Marie Hake and Kelly Eileen Hake combine their writing and research with authors Sally Laity and Dianna Crawford of northern California.

Historical, paperback, 352 pages, 5 ³/₁₆" x 8"